P9-DOD-250

Free

Free

and other stories

ANIKA NAILAH

DOUBLEDAY

New York   London   Toronto   Sydney   Auckland

PUBLISHED BY DOUBLEDAY
a division of Random House, Inc.
1540 Broadway, New York, New York 10036

DOUBLEDAY and the portrayal of an anchor with a dolphin
are trademarks of Doubleday, a division of Random
House, Inc.

Library of Congress Cataloging-in-Publication Data
Nailah, Anika.
Free and other stories / Anika Nailah.—1st ed.
p.   cm.
1. United States—Social life and customs—Fiction.
2. African Americans—Fiction. I. Title: Half title: Free.
II. Title.

PS3614.A56 F74 2002
813'.6—dc21
2001047572

ISBN 0-385-50293-1

Printed in the United States of America

February 2002

Book design by Donna Sinisgalli.

First Edition

10   9   8   7   6   5   4   3   2   1

Dedicated to

the first two characters

I ever met—

my mother and father.

A c k n o w l e d g m e n t s

First and foremost, I thank the Higher Power that gave me the faith and strength to complete this journey. To all my blood relatives and in-laws near and far, who have supported and encouraged this little girl who had a dream so long ago— WE DID IT!! A special thanks to my brother, Ernie, and my sisters, Leslie and Marcia, who always believed in me; my mother, who was my first editor and fan; and my father, who doesn't read fiction, but is proud of me anyway. (Hey, Dad, give this one a try. You might like it.) Thanks to my fellow artist, best friend, and husband, and my brilliantly creative son, Malcolm, for all the times I had to ignore you both to get this done.

To Warren Glass, thank you for exposing me to great literature, especially Ellison. To Megan, Jacqui, Kate, Diane, Susan P., and Earnest W., who know why. To Pam Bernstein, my agent, thank you for recognizing my abilities and opening the floodgates. To Janet Hill, who has forever spoiled me for all editors who may follow her, thanks for your professionalism, your patience, and your sisterhood. And a warm thank you to the entire Doubleday team.

To all of my friends who are thrilled to death for me—your joy keeps me going! (There are too many of you to name, so please forgive me for not listing all of you individually. You'll just have to be mad at me.) To all of my writing buddies in all the workshops I have been in over the years, you are my midwives. Congratulations. It's a book! To the twenty-five individuals who volunteered their time and brain cells to read this and give me feedback before I sent it out—I love you!

Thanks to my Books of Hope family for loving me enough to let me follow my path. We are rising together. To anyone anywhere who has helped me in thought or action to become a writer, consider yourself acknowledged.

Finally, I thank you, John O., for touching my life and watching over me. You done good.

Contents

Free

Passion is not friendly . . .
It contains an unspeakable hope.

—James Baldwin

It was raining down there on earth, but the sun was shining up in heaven. Two brown angels were talking, Old Angel and Young One.

"All kinds of free, boy," Old Angel said.

"What you mean?" Young One asked.

"Well, there's free to do something. Then there's free not to do something else. There's free of and free from."

"From what?"

"All kindsa things. Fear. Pain. White folks . . ."

"Free from white folks?"

"No, son. What I was trying to say is white folks ain't free either."

"They ain't?"

"Just look down there." His wrinkled finger pointed past the clouds. "All through the years. All those people. Different colors. Now look close. With your angel eyes, boy. Look at some of the

1

white ones. See how they spirits all knotted up from the inside? Some of 'em so crippled, they skin on the outside can't help 'em. You study that. 'Cuz when all is said and done, this here"—Old Angel gently touched Young One's soft, brown cheek—"don't mean a thing."

Trudy

Boston: 1954

"You cheated me out of fifty cents," the pillbox hat white woman said, sniffing indignantly, anxiously awaiting the scent of a lie.

"No, ma'am," Trudy said, motioning to the next customer. It was a busy Saturday at the store. She'd been on her feet all day.

"You're lyin'!"

"Ma'am, if you have a complaint, I suggest you take it up with the manager."

"What's his name? Where is . . . ?"

"Mr. Alcott."

At that very moment, Mr. Alcott's hefty belly was guiding him down the canned goods aisle, near the front of the store. He was in search of a stock number the boy he'd hired in desperation yesterday could not find. His ears, trained to pick up the grumblings of a dissatisfied customer from any corner of the store, heard bits and pieces of a conversation at Register 3.

". . . ignorant, obstinate . . ."

". . . Don't put your hands . . ."

". . . can't even count . . . got no business . . ."

". . . warning you, ma'am . . ."

Immediately, he realized this was not a dialogue to miss. After all the talk lately surrounding the Negro Question, due to that Supreme Court decision a month ago in Kansas, the last thing he needed was a race riot in his store. He straightened up as best he could. Tightening his belt around his unwieldy monument to good eating, he smoothed back what was left of his auburn hair, and approached Register 3.

He found two women—one tall, cinnamon; one salt-colored, bony. A crowd had formed. The white woman was old, small. She'd wedged herself into the cramped register space where Trudy stood. Alcott knew that Negro and white eyes were watching.

"Trudy," he said.

She turned. Her lips tightly pursed, nostrils wide, eyes wild past any recognition of the quiet Negro woman she usually was.

In the war, Alcott had seen fear turn a man's face inside out. But this look on Trudy Dillard's face was something different, fearless, decided.

"Trudy."

"Mr. Alcott," she answered.

"What seems to be the problem here?"

The white woman's sharp blue eyes cut the side of Alcott's face. "*I'm* the customer. *I'm* the customer. Why don't you ask *me* what the problem is?"

"Ma'am . . . ?" Alcott began.

6

"Thief. Plain and simple. That's what she is."

Trudy looked her in the eye. "I have neither need nor desire to steal anything from the likes of you."

"You impertinent . . . This how you train your colored girls?"

"Excuse me, ladies," Alcott said, squeezing his way in between them. He looked at the dollar figures standing at attention in the glass of the cash register. "How much was your purchase, ma'am?"

"Right here. Says right here"—the woman pressed her fingers against the register, a few inches from his nose—"fifteen dollars and fifty cents."

Alcott looked cautiously over at Trudy. She stood expressionless, arms crossed, eyes focused elsewhere.

"Well," Alcott tried again, "how much did the customer give you?"

"Sixteen dollars!" the woman yelled, dumping the contents of her brown paper bag on the counter. "This is what I bought. This is what I bought. Y'see?" She put her face close to his and leaned in. "The girl . . ." she said. Alcott could smell licorice on her breath. ". . . cheated me out of my money is all there is to it."

Trudy stepped out from behind the register, silent as death. Her arms at her sides, eyes locked on the white woman's. The crowd tensed.

Alcott wanted to touch Trudy's shoulder. Easy. Calm down.

Everything will be . . . He knew better. This white woman was a magnet, pulling Trudy to her like a razor. If a Negro hit a white woman, some white man would feel compelled to jump in. Then all hell would surely break loose. And when the dust cleared, Alcott would be left without the store he'd worked so hard to build, not to mention his best Negro worker.

He tried to reason. "Trudy. Think about your daughter."

Trudy didn't care anymore. If she had made a mistake with the change, it was too late. This woman had pushed her past apology. She was a human being. Sick of these damn white people saying and doing whatever they pleased. Sick of 'em all the time treating her like she got as much feeling as a piece of trash in the gutter. Like they did Mama. Like they did Daddy.

That night. One year back from fighting the war. Standing in the hallway. Only crime was walking the street looking for work. She remembered him cleaning off the egg that covered him from head to toe, a thin trickle of his blood mixing with white and yellow slime, running from the corner of his eye, down the side of his face. She remembered hating his patience when he told her, "Daddy's alright, baby. Eggs. That's all. Just eggs."

Sick of these white folks. Sick. Of every last one.

The white woman looked at the colored girl's face. *Yeah,*

go ahead, she thought. *Police'll be all over you so fast you won't know what hit you.*

There was a short distance between the woman's face and Trudy's hand. It would be quick. Her brown hand, the red mark, that white skin.

Something stopped her.

Maybe it was the hint of a smile on the woman's lips, or the resigned expressions of the Negroes around her. And what *would* her half-grown daughter do without her? Negroes were being burned, beaten, and killed without a second thought.

The anger encased her, freezing the soles of her shoes to the floor. She could feel everything climbing to the top of her head, then stopping, icing over into one solid block. She concentrated on it. Tried to free it, let it loose, move on. Instead, she felt the ice catch in her throat. She knew this block well. It belonged to her. She would hide it, protect the precious tears it held. Dissolve it, piece by piece, when she was alone. Trudy saw herself, slowly, recrossing her arms, turning away. She heard the cash register ring.

The sweaty palm of Mr. Alcott's hand held two quarters. He offered them to the white woman.

"Um-hmm. Knew I was right." She walked toward Trudy. "I *demand* an apology."

Trudy walked past her. This woman no longer existed. She had tried to snatch Trudy through the wall that separated

9

them, Negro from white. Wanted to see this colored girl broken, handcuffed on the other side. She had failed.

"Next," Trudy said, stepping inside her register area,
smiling at a new customer, "I'm open."

"Hmph. This isn't over." The white woman gathered her
bags and moved toward the door. "I promise you that, gal."

The perspiration that had dribbled down the hills of
Alcott's body and collected in the valleys, now floated freely
down the trails of his face, back, chest, and arms, as he
watched the crowd unfurl, returning the old woman to the
world outside his store.

Four

1 . Gumbo

The madness followed him out of the house as he walked down Clover Street in Murrayville. The familiar tightening of his back, the pulsing muscles in his legs and feet, signs that the madness was upon him, close enough to jump him, wrestle him to the ground.

He took off. Some guys were on the corner singing.

Oh-oh, yes, I'm the great pretender.

He headed for Matthews Park, eight blocks down. His tennis shoes came down hard against the street, the beige soles of his feet pressing white, deep, searching for the grooves, for the grooves, to propel him, save him from the terror. The madness clawed at him, barely missing the white of his T-shirt. His chest was sore from the hammering of his breath against his rib cage. Sweat cut one path after another from his forehead down his lean, teenage body. His mouth was dry.

When at last he reached the park, Gumbo was bent over. His hands were on his knees. He felt the madness tire and leave him, his breath, in gasps, return to him. He sensed the madness following its trail back to Clover Street. He saw it transform into a spidery mist, then slip quietly under the front door of his house, taking its time, as it settled, back into the corners of every room.

Gumbo had outrun it one more time. As he sat down, he watched the brown spots his tears and sweat made in the dirt. He felt heat come through his wet T-shirt as he leaned against a concrete wall.

Five months ago, the madness had taken his sister, Marion. She'd left Murrayville for New York with two boys from the church choir. They'd decided they could sing that "worldly" music. Get a record pressed. Become famous.

While she was gone, sunlight broke through the blinds in her room. Each night, darkness chased it away. The madness sat on her windowsill, content to wait for her return.

Marion finally came back. She was good, better than she'd imagined. She really had something. All the A&R people at the labels said they could make her a star. She only had to *want* the dream.

She went from 125 pounds to 260, feeding on all the pieces of herself she loathed and feared. The door knocked. The phone called. Letters jammed themselves in the space beneath her door. Pretty flowers died in brittle bunches on the other side. She answered nothing, snuck out to quickly spend her New York money on whatever she could stuff in shopping bags, washed herself from time to time, and slept.

The madness had her on a leash. She never stayed gone too long.

Just last week, the madness had come for Richard Preston, Gumbo's daddy. When he couldn't get out of bed that morning, his wife, Maureen, dragged, half carried him to the doctor's, temporarily outwitting the madness, as it hunted Preston through the smell of his despair. Was it in his navy workpants draped flawlessly across the back of the armchair? Inside the toes of his leather slippers? Or maybe it just lay forgotten beneath the sheets, between him and Maureen, since the children had been born.

Preston was a tall, dark Negro with a deep laugh, and an opinion about everything. Part of The Brotherhood most his life. Honest work, being a porter. The money wasn't nothing to be ashamed of neither, thanks to Mr. A. Philip Randolph.

Always moving. Trains taking him this place and that. At first, he liked it, understood how necessary the motion was to rock the thing inside him that was soft and scared. After a while, all that moving began to bother him. Someone else was doing it and he all the time going in whatever direction they told him. Buying a house was his way of yanking himself back, having somewhere to put his feet besides a sooty depot everytime he got off the train, somewhere that was standing still, somewhere with his name on it.

Then he laid eyes on Maureen. Saw exactly what his house was missing. Knew right away he wanted to make lots of pretty brown babies that looked just like her. Lord, did he love him some Maureen. Not one day went by when he didn't poke fun at her. Couldn't help himself, so crazy about her. He was a little boy on the playground all over again, messing with some cute girl he really wanted to kiss.

She said, "Yes." She moved in. She filled out. The house filled up. Their happiness, a fancy piece of chocolate they swallowed whole.

They never noticed when the melting began. The sweetness lingering to tease the memory. Preston by himself on the road, riding those trains. He'd come around exhausted, two days at a time. Then, he was gone. Maureen would stand in the living room, her back to the door. She would breathe in the scent of him he'd left behind. At night, after the babies were asleep, she'd hug his bathrobe against her nakedness, beneath the covers, her cheek against the skin of his pillow, breathing in the scent of him until he returned.

That morning, years later, when all the babies were grown, and Preston could not make it out of bed, the doctor told Maureen her husband was fine. There was nothing wrong with his legs. Richard Preston never told her he had been hiding from the madness for as long as he could remember.

That particular morning, he was just plain tired. He had

run his race. That morning, he had finally decided to quit running.

A long time ago, Preston had told his nine-year-old son, Gumbo, how the madness ate people up in all kinds of ways. How when Preston was four, in the summertime, he'd seen it jump into his own father's hands and nearly strangle the life out of his mama, that day Grandpa got laid off. Gumbo didn't say much. Just looked at him with that little man expression. His silent fight against the fear his daddy was causing in the bottom of his stomach. Preston told Gumbo about that early spring, when he was twelve and saw the madness in the eyes of broken men standing on the corners, sneaking sips from back pockets, thinking no one saw, not caring if someone did. Preston was a young man when he recognized the madness in himself. Something about the way he felt when he woke up, a rhythm he fought to find to take him from the bedroom to the end of his day. Just doing, not feeling.

Gumbo hadn't understood exactly what his father was trying to tell him back then. He knew his daddy laughed an awful lot and tried to make him laugh whenever something hurt. Either way, Gumbo figured sooner or later, the madness would catch him too. He'd smelled its rancid breath, heard it whisper "Fuck it" in his ear while he was in school. Gumbo's plan was to run and keep running as far away from Clover Street as he could get. When he got tired of running, he would sing. It would begin in his head, a memory of an

17

old-time 78 Mama had put on the record player when Pop was at work.

Why not take all of me?

Mama turning, slowly, her toes digging into the shaggy carpet. Her eyes closed. One hand clutching her waist. The other, fingers spread, reaching.

Gumbo could see her, hear the tune, if he kept himself in darkness, shut everything else out. It became a hum, vibrating through his nose and cheeks, unfolding in his throat into notes that hooked one into the other and rose bravely from his full lips, reaching. Reaching for that space, high above him, beyond the blue.

2. Jimmy

He paid the bus driver and looked for a seat.

"Jimmy!"

It was Anna. She was sitting with Terry, Mary, and Frances. They were all wearing their blue and yellow Wordsworth High School colors in their blouses, skirts, and bobby socks.

"I thought that was you," Anna said, with her brash, blue-eyed smile, as Jimmy walked toward them.

These Park Ridge white girls always made him nervous,

especially the pretty ones. He wondered if they did it on purpose. Did they know about the heat simmering across his cheeks, the sweat that was beginning to drip from his armpits down the sides of his body? One on one was difficult enough, but when you got them all together in a group, they were like the big defensive tackles he'd faced many times—muscles twitching, ready to corner and sack him as soon as he caught the pass.

"Hey," he managed.

They giggled, half self-consciously, half impishly.

Anna patted the seat next to her.

"Where you goin'?" Terry asked, her dark brown bangs hanging above her green eyes.

"Barber shop," he mumbled.

"Where?" Frances probed, all freckles.

"Yeah. What barber shop is over this way? Besides, what's wrong with the shop in town?" Anna added, flinging her long, blond hair to the side.

"Nothin'. I just go downtown."

"In Murrayville?" Mary asked, amazement showing in her plain, intelligent face. Her father would never allow her to go there, girlfriends or not.

"Yeah." The sweat was forming above his top lip.

"Why?" Mary persisted. "Why would *anyone* want to go into Murrayville?"

Jimmy wanted to run off the bus. He was trapped. At times like this he hated his mother for moving to Park Ridge. He knew it wasn't her fault. They'd given her a job at the army base a few miles north of this town, and here he was. Jimmy stammered his way through. "It's . . . they . . . it's . . . they don't know how to cut my hair in the barber shop in town."

He was too embarrassed to explain how uncomfortable the white men in the Park Ridge shop had made him feel that day, staring at him with that what-the-hell-you-doing-in-here-boy look on their faces.

"That's ridiculous," Anna said, her fingers finding their way through the soft meadow on his head. "Hair is hair," she continued, a few breaths away from his Negro lips.

Jimmy fought the strange sensations flowing through him and stared at the white ceiling of the bus.

Terry followed Anna's lead and began to squeeze his hair between her thumb and other fingers. "I don't know. It does feel a little different." She laughed.

Negro and white adults were watching.

"C'mon. Cut it out." Jimmy gently pulled his head away.

Anna enjoyed the attention.

Bad enough everyone knew who he was. There hadn't ever been an All-American Negro running back at Wordsworth. But this could get him killed. Only God knew what conversations would come up around family dinner tables that night. He pulled the cord. "This is my stop," he breathed, standing up, "See ya later."

"Bye, Jimmy," Anna whispered, winking. "See ya around."

He didn't look back to watch the bus pull away. He knew they'd be staring. He also knew that Anna never acted like that when her boyfriend, Danny, was around. It was like Jimmy was a black furry thing she could play with, a stuffed animal she could touch any way she wanted to. The thing of it was, he liked her touching him, and she knew it.

Step by step, Jimmy began to walk with his head up. The shame he felt in the town he had come from, dissolving into the air of the place where he was now. Each step closer to the barber shop, gathering him, bringing him closer to himself.

All of these emotions were so confusing. He'd wished his father back alive more times than he could count. But all he had was the black and white snapshot he kept in his wallet of a man who looked like him, his brown muscled chest, his cheeks sucked in, as he pulled hard on the cigarette between his lips. Then there was the shot of him in full uniform, with all the other soldiers, standing straight, looking ahead. Mama said they'd called it "The Good War," because whenever old white men took a notion to have something that didn't belong to them, they got young men to kill other young men for it, and they called it good.

Jimmy wondered if his daddy knew how much he would need him. Did his daddy have the same questions about white girls and Negroes on his mind when he was a boy? Did his daddy think of him in that moment before the grenade scattered him across the trees and dirt so far away from home? Jimmy tried to get inside this man he never knew, wear his cocoa skin, stretch his smile across his face, feel the blood enter and leave his heart. He strained to imagine how his daddy might explain, in ways Mama couldn't, all these dreams he was having about Anna.

In most of them, she would pull him on top of her, placing his ebony hand on her sunless breast, and smile. Entering her was always the same. He was crashing, bursting into a world that could never let him in. This world held him tight, loved his black ass. Believed he could make everything he touched sweeter than it could ever hope to be.

He was touching Anna. She loved him. She was white and she loved him.

Since I met you baby, all I need is you . . .

Jimmy breathed a sigh of relief. He could hear the music and smell the smells. He could see the red and white symbol of Sam's Barber Shop turning in the glass. He crossed the street.

3 . T - B o n e

"Boy you bet' come back on down here and eat your breakfast," Gramma Bowen was saying. It was the third time this week. T-Bone had once again found himself outside of his body, looking down at himself and his grandmother sharing a meal at the kitchen table. The edge in her voice jarred him, and he came back in. He seemed to be getting less and less control over it. It just happened all of a sudden, with not so much as a here-we-go-again. He'd learned not to fight it.

This thing that he had was a gift. Some old folks said he'd been born with a veil, an extra layer of skin across his face that helped him sense things. He wasn't afraid of it anymore. But it had terrified his mother. Now she had four other little ones to care for. Didn't need no strange one who could play tricks with space and time. Looked too much like his daddy, Marcus, anyway, who she hadn't seen since the night he put T-Bone inside her.

Marcus was lean. He wasn't handsome, but women found him attractive. Had some kind of strange energy he had no better use for than making women fall in love with him. Then it'd get too much for him and he'd have to disappear.

T-Bone's mama was cute in a tough kind of way. Marcus had never intended on staying with her long. Too hardheaded. But she sure looked like flowing moonlight that night in her silky white dress.

Miss Bowen had warned her daughter about him. She'd heard all kind of stories (in church, no less) about this brazen-as-sin man who ended up in all sorts of women's beds—young, old, married, or otherwise. Course the girl didn't listen. Turned up pregnant and pitiful. When trying to beat the child out of her didn't work, Miss Bowen had no choice but to cozy up to the cold fact that she was going to be a grandmother at thirty-four, to a child who had no father.

Gramma Bowen knew about the baby's gift. She'd seen it in him early, recognized it. She'd had it too, when she was young and Murrayville was nothing but woods. She had learned to hide it. Everytime it showed up, her mama whipped it out of her with a fresh switch. A sign of the devil. One day, her mama finally ran the thing bloody and whimpering into the forest.

That was how Gramma Bowen knew all about it. So when her daughter told her about T-Bone's ways, she was more than willing to take the child in and raise him as her own. She knew exactly what to do.

What Gramma didn't realize was exactly how powerful T-Bone's piece of magic was. No matter how she tried to scare it out of him, it just kept shape-changing into something else. Never seen a devil spirit like this one before. Made the boy's cells keep multiplying like some kind of cancer, all through his muscles and joints, pulling him out to a six-foot-nine-inch frame at sixteen. Then, it had the nerve to make him smart. Showed itself in all kinds of tests—IQ, arithmetic, reading, even telepathy.

The teachers at school had him special tested again, just to be sure. Except for Miss Turner, the only Black teacher and the toughest, most of them had little faith in the intelligence of "these Murrayville children." They looked at T-Bone's blue-black face. This couldn't be. But it could and it was. The test papers said "Richard Waters" (better known as "T-Bone") was a bona fide genius. His buddy, Blood, had told him that long before any tests.

But school was a place to sleep or act crazy, certainly nowhere to think, especially once you realized they couldn't answer your questions. And T-Bone *had* some questions. He was a black lighthouse, trying to break through his darkness, shining on whatever pleased him at the moment. He couldn't connect with the place his teachers said his people came from. It was full of wild animals, half-naked men, and women who screamed and showed their breasts. The only other thing they'd ever done, according to the history books he was given, was line up and become slaves. T-Bone had some questions. He needed answers.

One day, out of boredom, he discovered that the gift had expanded itself into his diaphragm. He discovered he had a

talent for singing. No one thought much of his sudden interest in joining the school chorus.

Until they heard him sing.

Mr. Tierney, the director, still tells the story. His eyes
just kept looking upward, past T-Bone's thighs, to his chest,
to his throat, to his lips, to his forehead, until they stayed
fixed upon some point above T-Bone's head. In all his years
as a music teacher, he had never experienced tones so sweet.
They made his eyelids shut tightly, as the tears slowly slid
down his cheeks and into his mustache.

T-Bone was floating blind, in control. He had found a
way to make the gift his own; a breathtaking silk scarf that
kept coming from his throat, each color more exciting than
the last—deeper, richer, softer, stronger.

4. Blood

His almond knuckles were still ragged and sore from
yesterday. Blood danced a boxer's dance, his short shadow
boxing back at him from the brick wall of the campgrounds.
He could go. He could duke. He couldn't wait to feel the new
soreness, the fresh blows against his chest. Sonny O'Connor
would be at the top of the hill soon.

It had started as *nigger whiteboy yo mama let'sdothis*. It
had become a love dance at sunset. The two boys snuck out of
their cabins every day after supper so they could fight. Sky

against earth. Day against night. Words long ago forgotten. The fight was the thing. Speed, taking the punch, the perfect blow, the way the body felt in motion or in pain. These were the things that counted.

Blood looked up and saw Sonny running toward him, down the side of the hill. Everything started pumping. They eyed each other and walked silently into the grassy meadow. Dukes up. They circled.

Grunt. Blood dug right in. Sonny's jawbone. Left jab. Gently. Can't leave too many marks.

Size the nigger up. Shoulders. Shoulders. Graziano. Snap the fist. Find the hole. Just like Uncle Jerry does it. *Grunt.* Yeah. Block. Angle. Sonny looked for hesitation, signs of some undigested thought. Blood's cheek. *Grunt.* Bam.

Fired up. I'ma kick this white boy's ass tonight. Sweet Sugar Ray. Show me what you got. Dance. Bob. To the body. Solid. Blood's mother, dressed like a whore, flashed across his mental screen. *Come to mama, baby.* Bam.

Grunt. Air. Air. Good one. Sonny pushed his soot-black hair away from his eyes. *Grunt.* Duck.

Wha'sa matter? Give your mama a . . . Shit. Red dripping from Blood's nose. *Ain't got no mama.* Bam. *Grunt.* Bam. Sonny's chest. Bam. *Reform school. Grunt. Never knew my daddy.* Bam.

Blood on Sonny's shirt. Lip split. Weave. Bam. Block.

Grunt. Knuckles bleeding. *Grunt*. Stay up. Stay up. Out of breath. *Grunt*. Keep movin'. *O-oh*. Pretty. Ribs throbbin'. Hurtin' good.

Enough. Enough.

Breathing heavy, Sonny lifted his shirt. There was blood on it.

"You fine," Blood said, wincing. "Better keep your shirt off." He lifted his own.

"That one don't look good." Sonny reached for the red on Blood's chest.

"Don't touch it."

"What we gonna tell 'em?"

"I be alright."

"You sure?"

"Wipe your mouth."

"See ya around."

Blood washed his face in the water fountain. He'd need a day to heal this time. He hoped he looked presentable enough to crawl into bed without being noticed.

Darkness hid him as he walked, slowly, past the evening trees, to his cabin. The other boys were too busy using their precious few minutes before lights out to pay him any mind. He flopped onto his bottom bunk bed and lay on his back, his short legs stretched out in front of him. The lights went out. Too tired to get undressed, he began to nod off. His eyelids were getting weak, fighting off his dreams. Didn't want no dreams. Too many faces he didn't know, didn't want to know, showing up in alleyways he didn't want to walk down. He fell out staring at the grass stains on his sneakers, concentrating on a melody.

C'mon, baby, let the good times roll . . .

All night long.

5 . August Dance

The sun had risen triumphantly over the camp and blessed the day. Five wooden cabins held the one hundred and seventy boys who lived here every summer on these twenty-eight acres of evergreen woods, baseball fields, lakes, and ponds. By late afternoon, each cabin was thick with boys wrapped waist down in towels, standing in front of mirrors, frowning at pimples, Pine Sol in their nostrils, combing, slicking, parting their hair. Some were playing cards with each other on army blanketed beds. Others were ironing their pants. The floors shined. Everything was ready for the visitors who were coming to the Annual August Dance.

That evening when Blood was in the shower, he secretly touched his sore spots. He dried off, then shined his loafers, put a military crease in his chinos, and checked his do. He covered the bruises on his cheek and hands with a few small Band-Aids. He was clean.

Blood walked out of his cabin to where the dance was going to be. On the way, he remembered that T-Bone would be coming. He always came for the August Dance. So did most of Murrayville. There was always plenty of fried chicken, potato salad, burgers, hot dogs, and big, deep barrels filled with ice cubes and soda pop.

"Blood!"

It was T-Bone.

"Hey, man." He checked T-Bone out and nodded. "You lookin' sharp, T."

"Uh-huh. Am I too early? Damn. What happened to you?"

"Got in a scuffle with a white boy . . . you know. The band almost ready."

"Hope these boys can do it. I want to float outta here tonight, baby. Gramma kickin' my butt."

" 'Bout what?"

"School."

"Aw, man. School's easy for you. Now this here camp, wish it could last forever."

They stood on line to get something to eat. All kinds of girls were everywhere in tight, little groups with their skirts, made-up faces, and hair bows. The bolder ones had gone off into the bushes to sneak a cigarette or a kiss. Some smiled.

Others looked away. T-Bone and Blood brought their filled-up plates to a spot under a tree. Between bites, they talked in low tones about the girls passing by and what they could do for them. In his head, Blood was replaying last night's fight, countering the punches he didn't block in time.

"Hear something?" T-Bone asked, jerking him out of his thoughts.

"Naw. Wait. Yeah. Singin'. Somebody singin'. C'mon."

Blood and T-Bone walked a few feet toward the lake. Hand-holding couples were beginning to form. Eyebrow-raising counselors were stationed here and there. A few of the guys were hanging around near the water, playing with a tune.

In the still of the night . . .

They stopped.

"Come on, Gumbo. You not hittin' that note, man," one of them said.

"Alright. Alright."

They sang again. The one called Gumbo was smiling now. He was closing his eyes. T-Bone couldn't resist. He jumped on in and wrestled for the lead. A short guy gave him a menacing look, then walked away. He couldn't compete with what T-Bone was layin' down.

Gumbo's eyes lit up. More people gathered 'round.

T-Bone motioned to Blood to join in. Blood hung back, until he saw all the girls getting high off the sound. He threw his voice in and the whole thing got fat. Fat and strong. Soon, it was just the three of them, crooning pure, thick honey.

After the second song, Blood shook his head. "Something's missing."

"You kiddin'?" T-Bone asked.

"Naw. I'm tellin' you. We need somethin'."

"What you mean?" Gumbo asked.

"A bottom." Blood smiled. "Yeah. Bass man." He'd been watching a square-looking cat whose eyes had been asking if he could be part of the happening.

"Hey man, you sing?" Blood asked him.

"Little bit," Jimmy answered.

"Hey. Ain't you that All-American play for Wordsworth?" T-Bone asked.

"Yeah."

"Jimmy . . . ?"

"Jimmy Collins," Jimmy said, extending his hand, smelling of a mixture of dime store cologne and nerves.

"Yeah." T-Bone smiled, gesturing to the others. "This here's Blood. This, Gumbo, right?"

"Uh-huh." Gumbo nodded. "Can you sing bass?"

Jimmy shrugged. "I'll give it a try."

They sang all night. Evening brought a breeze off the lake

and a crowd that grew larger and larger. Guys in the band even came outside to listen. Blood kept the melody moving. Gumbo stroked it easy. Jimmy held it together. T-Bone made it soar. The music was father to them all, as they were brother to each other.

Their sound grew wider, brighter. They were hitting the notes straight through the center. The music made some people cry. It lifted them up. These four had come to the dance looking for one thing, and something else found them. Each song helped them to create an each other they couldn't make on their own.

"You alright, Jimmy," Blood said, giving him some skin.

"You too, man."

"One more, fellas," T-Bone pleaded.

"You a singin' fool, T." Gumbo laughed.

They sang one more. They pushed it out, up, over, around. Swam in it. Walked in it. Turned it inside out, upside down, 'til six brown hands opened to let T-Bone, like a bird, fly free. He broke out, high, above the three. And then his heart reached back, pulled them, Gumbo, Blood, and Jimmy—one bright ribbon, up, with him. They all hung on and floated there as long as they could, smoothin', soothin'.

My Side of the Story

"Sweetheart. My beautiful, strong son. I made this tape so you could understand why I had to leave. I want so much for you to understand. Last night, as I was taking my suitcases down the stairs, I peeked into your bedroom and I cried, because I knew I couldn't take you with me . . ."

Ma left us in the spring. I miss her real bad. Now it's fall and we're moving. I don't want to move. But what I want doesn't matter. No one ever asks me what I want.

I am only eleven.

I stand about five feet four inches tall, three inches of which is my Afro. Ma calls me a walking fudgesicle because she says I have a sweet complexion, like her. Real modest.

Right now, I'm supposed to be packing, but I'm sitting on the floor of my room with this tape machine Dad used in the old days. I'm listening to Ma's voice. It's like a Ping Pong ball going back and forth against my empty blue walls.

"What can I tell you to make you understand? You think I've abandoned you. I'm your mother. I'm supposed to be there no matter what. You may even hate me . . ."

I have to bring the last box of my stuff downstairs so Dad can put it in the car. Then it's my job to put Malcolm's leash on and get him in the backseat. Malcolm's the color of ashes sort of dropped all over a white sheet, and he has a black patch on the top of his head and on the tip of his tail. And he has eyes like my foggy green marbles.

Ma used to talk about how weird the two of us look together early in the morning. Me, I'm half asleep, but my hair is standing up like I stuck my finger in a wall socket. I can barely keep my eyes open, but Malcolm, his eyes are real wide, like they're trying to catch the sun, kind of golden green. Spooky.

The day after Ma left, she called to tell me she still loved me and everything. I was snotting and crying all over myself, begging her to come back. But she just kept saying she couldn't. I was so mad, I told her I didn't love her and never wanted to see her again anyway. Then she started crying. But I didn't care. I wanted to hurt her. I mean, she just left. She didn't even tell me.

One morning she was there and we had grits and eggs and sausage like every other day before when I went to school and Dad went to the city. And the next day she was gone.

And school was dumber than usual because I didn't even care that my teacher, Miss Zimmerman, was the ugliest white woman I had ever seen or that I was the only Black kid in the class or that the Greeks and Romans had nothing to do with what Dad told me really happened back then. I didn't even care that some kids were laughing at me because I was crying, right there in the middle of the history lesson.

Miss Zimmerman came over and put her ugly face in mine and started asking me all these stupid questions like was I sick or was there something wrong. I couldn't talk but just kept crying as she took my hand and walked me out into the hall, telling everyone to be quiet and keep still 'til she got back. She offered me a snot handkerchief from her dress pocket, but I told her that was okay thanks. I could hardly see her by the time we got outside, which wasn't so bad.

She kept looking at me from behind those cat glasses. Finally, after saying nothing and smiling like her cheeks were lifting weights, she told me I could stay outside in the hallway until I felt like coming back to class.

White people are so simple sometimes when they don't know what to say or feel sorry for you because you're Black and crying about something you can't explain to nobody.

"Things will be different now. But I will always love you. You have to believe that . . ."

At first, I couldn't play this tape. It hurt too much. It still makes me sad, but now when I play it, it makes me feel kind of like Ma is still here. Like her telling me everything's gonna be alright.

"EDDIE!"

It's Dad.

"Eddie! Turn that thing off and get down here."

"I'm coming, Dad."

"Don't make me come up there and drag you downstairs, boy."

Uh-oh. He's sounding real Black. That means he's mad. The only time he sounds Black is when he gets mad. Like when he argued with Ma. Any other time he'd say something like "I beg to differ with you." As soon as they started fighting, he'd say, "Girl, what the hell you talkin' 'bout?"

"Okay. Okay, Dad. I'm coming."

Sometimes I'm so mad I hate everybody and I feel like I don't want to see Ma. Other times I miss her so much I want to cry. I can't figure it out. And I can't talk to Dad about it because he has a new girlfriend, Liz, a real winner, who follows him around like a vacuum cleaner trying to suck up some dirt. What's wrong with him? Doesn't he miss Ma too? It's like he never even loved her. Nothing makes any sense, like the reason why we're moving. It's all Grandma's fault. I was there when she talked Dad into it.

I was listening at the top of the stairs. Grandma and Dad were in the living room. Grandma has blue hair. For real.

She's very light-skinned, short, and fat. And when she moves, she looks like a teardrop trying to walk. She was moving closer to the couch where Dad was sitting.

He was leaning his head back against the white pillows, the way he taught me to do when I had a bloody nose or something. Both of his hands were covering his eyes. Dad has the biggest hands in the world. Malcolm used to sleep in them when he was a puppy. He's tall too, but something made him look kind of little to me that night. His potbelly looked big. It was making his red bathrobe bulge open, and the curly, gray hairs on his chest were showing. They looked like foam or something against his root-beer skin.

"She won't find another man out there who'll take care of her like I did," he was saying.

"Put some lead in your spine, son," Grandma said. "Let Linda go." She sat next to him.

"After all I did for her. After everything . . ."

"People like her make a living out of finding folk just like you." She moved his hand like he was a little boy, and put it under hers. "Probably ran off with some bright-eyed, empty-head young boy who doesn't know any better. When he unwraps all that pretty paper, he'll see what he has. Snake."

"Mama, please don't start that again."

"When you married her, I tried to help her out. Bad upbringing. Her people living all up under each other in Harlem. Eating that greasy food. Drinking and carrying on. Acting just like the niggers white folks say we are."

"Before she . . . left, she was good to me. Maybe it was me. Maybe. I don't know. I just didn't know how to make her happy. I couldn't make her happy, Mama."

"You made her happy, alright. Gave her a beautiful home, nice clothes. She was happy."

"She walked away. Left everything."

"Tried to take your soul."

"Twenty years." His eyes filled up and looked around the room. "She left me, Mama." Then he started crying like a baby.

And this is the sickening part. Dad was just shaking his head, when Grandma made him lay down in her lap, and she kissed the side of his face like he was a little kid or something. That's when she let him have it.

"You got to move, William." She wiped his tears with her hands and looked into his face. "Can't make a new path with old shoes."

So that's why we're moving. Seems to me it would have been a whole lot cheaper if Grandma just bought us all new shoes. But she didn't. Like I told you, nobody asks me anything. I'm supposed to just get up and go.

Well, I can't. I've lived here since I was a baby. There used to be pictures on my wall, to brainwash me into being smart and stuff, like the one with the pitiful little, purple guy with a pointy skull who talked about how much fun it was to read. I figured if reading made you look like he did, it wasn't worth it. Then there was this other poster that took up one whole wall. It was like a giant cartoon of all these numbers that had arms and legs, and marched around like they were human. I guess it was supposed to help you learn how to count. I used to have nightmares about all of them chasing me, especially the eights, with their big eyes. Ma would have to come in and tell me a story until I fell back to sleep.

"EDDIE!"

Good-bye, purple man. Goodbye, room.

Dad is locking the door of the house for the last time. Grandma, me, and Malcolm are waiting for him in the car. Malcolm has no idea of what's going on. To get him to leave the backyard, I had to convince him that we were going to a better place.

When I told him, he sat down on the grass, real slow, and then he started sniffing with his wet, black nose. He tilted his head to one side, the way he does when he doesn't understand something, and his antenna ears poked up, into the sky, so he wouldn't miss a sound. He listened to all the junk I told him, and when I finished, he just sat there and looked at me. Finally, when I said, "Look, Malcolm, if you stay here, you'll starve," he stood up, ready to go.

Now he's starting to whine. I am whispering in his ear that everything is gonna be alright, but he keeps jumping up, putting both his paws on my shoulders so he can whine right in my face.

"Can't you keep that mutt quiet?" Grandma is saying, brushing his hairs off her shoulder.

Dad is getting in the car. Everyone is quiet. As we back out of the driveway and start going down the street, I look back at our brown and white house getting smaller and smaller, with the flower boxes we never used, and the metal milkbox by the door that Dad used to flip open so he could reach the cold, glass bottles of milk, and carry them into the kitchen. Everything is disappearing and there's nothing I can do about it. I'm so sick of crying. It doesn't stop anything from happening like it does when you're little.

I feel real tired. Malcolm and I go to sleep on each other. I don't remember what I dream about. I just feel like somebody cut me and let all my blood run out. The car stops. I think I have been sleeping a long time because the side of my face is all tickly with Malcolm's hairs. Something feels strange. Maybe it's the funny feeling I have in my throat, or the way the car stopped. All at once. Just like that. It stopped. Not like you're going along okay and you can take it stopping because you expect it to, but like all of a sudden you figure something out. Something there is no getting out of.

We have come to the new house.

It's uglier than Miss Zimmerman. It doesn't look anything like our old house. It's real big and probably is supposed to be white, but it just looks dirty to me. There's one of those statues on the lawn of a drunk guy with big red eyes, a mustache, a black hat, and a bottle of alcohol. Real classy.

I am just sitting in the backseat. Malcolm is real quiet, lying on my feet like how a cat curls up in front of a fireplace on those corny cards people send us at Christmas, only different. The two of us are just sitting there while Dad doesn't even notice, and jumps out of the car with a whole bunch of boxes. Grandma is already wobbling her way up the path to the door. She is happier than a hippo in a mudhole.

I'm about to get up, but I think it's too late. Liz is coming my way. She's skinny and has almost no hair on her head. Dad must have met her when he had one eye closed in a dark room. She is the color of burnt potato chips. And I guess she spent so much money on her makeup that she didn't have any left over for a good bra, because she is bouncing up and down in front so much that she is smacking herself in the face with her own chest. Now she's opening the car door, pulling me out, and slobbering kisses all over me.

I know that I'm going to hate it here.

For two weeks, I have lived in this crummy neighborhood. I guess Dad doesn't have to pay for everything now, so he doesn't care. And he can't be lonely, because no-hair

Hoover never leaves him alone. It's not like we're living in a shack or anything. Or that the other houses are beat-up or something. It's just that it's not *my* neighborhood. It's not *my* house. It's not the path I built with Dad with the gray and red rocks in it to walk on until you get to our front door, right before you pass the purple flowers Ma planted in the circle on the front lawn. Not to mention all the grass I helped Dad plant with that little red machine on wheels that spit all the seeds out into the dirt.

I don't belong here. It's like this movie I saw where this guy is the only human left. He's surrounded by these aliens from another planet, only they look just like he does. So he has to pretend he's one of them when he's really not.

Except for the one house that looks like it was built by some guy who was homesick for Transylvania, every house on this street looks the same. Every Saturday, these people all get up at the same time, put on the same clothes, and then walk outside at the same minute. Then they all go into their garages and get their lawnmowers. That's when they have dumb conversations over their fences like:

"Good morning, John."

"Good morning, Ted."

"How's the wife?" (Like she's the TV set he just got fixed.)

"Couldn't be better."

"We're having a few people over for cocktails next Friday. You and Joan *must* come by. There's this new antique table we bought. You've got to see it."

"Love to."

"Splendid. Friday then."

Then the guy without the table smiles until the cocktail guy goes back to pretending he's a gardener or something. But the no-table guy is really mad because he didn't buy anything new to show off to the cocktail guy. So the next Saturday he makes sure he has something.

Another thing is, they only let the mothers out of their houses during the day, so they can finish all the hard work before their husbands get home. All those guys probably do is carry their potbellies from the chairs in their offices, stuff them into their cars, and drive a hundred miles to get back to the same chair they fell asleep in the night before, right in front of their TV sets. Tough life. The women clean and shop and take care of the kids. If they're lucky, they have a chance to get bombed on whatever's in the liquor cabinet while their big kids are in school.

So that's the neighborhood.

The only thing I like about this place is the lake. Way down at the end of the street, after you pass all the ugly houses, there's a dead end. Right there is this real pretty lake. It's bright and blue. Sometimes ducks come and splash in it and sit around the edge of it. It's great. Whenever I go there, I don't feel like me. 'Cause it's peaceful and clear and you can forget stuff. It's like you can blend in with the water and disappear.

Most of the time, though, I have to stay by the house. Which is getting harder and harder to do. See, Liz has this dog named Caesar. He's big and black and there's two things he hates: white people and Malcolm. I mean, here he is, and nobody asked him anything like, "Do you want to live here?" or "How do you feel about sharing your backyard?" Nothing. They just brought him here to this white house in this white neighborhood and chained him to a tree. Then, even though he got used to being chained, he still figured the yard was his, when in plops this other dog he never saw before who runs up to him, pulling me at the other end of the leash, talking about let's be friends. 'Cause Malcolm didn't know any better. He was just happy to find someone he could talk to.

But I think Caesar scared Malcolm to death because he snarled and snapped and told him to stay the hell away from him. So I had to chain Malcolm to another tree on the other side of the yard. He whined and whined when I started to walk away like was I stupid or crazy or what to leave him all alone with this Tasmanian devil.

The point is, every day we've been here, Caesar's been barking and Malcolm's been whining. So people have been complaining that the dogs are making too much noise. Nobody is louder than the crazy guy in the Transylvania house with the jungle weeds who beats his wife every night. But none of these lawnmower guys has the guts to knock on his door and tell him to stop. They pick on two dogs who it isn't even their fault that they're here in the first place.

I was trying to explain that to Grandma the night the guy next door came by to say that the dogs were barking too much. He must have come straight from work because he was dressed up in his suit and tie and he had a briefcase in his hand. At first, I thought he was one of those guys who goes around telling people he used to be a sinner but now him and God are best friends, so buy this magazine. But he was worse.

After he left, Grandma said, "Your father's going to have to do something about those dogs."

So I said, "It's not their fault. Dogs are supposed to bark."

"That's not the point. We can't cause any trouble here. We have to show them that we're decent people. The dogs will just have to go."

"That's dumb. I know Dad won't let these stupid people—"

"Who do you think you're talking to, boy? If your mama had raised you right, you'd know better than to talk to me like that."

"Don't you talk about my mother."

Smack. Right across my face.

I hated her.

"It's time you faced the truth about your mother. She's the one who left, not your daddy. Don't walk away from me when I'm talking to you, boy."

She was still talking by the time I got upstairs and locked the door to my room.

I turned Ma's tape up real loud so I couldn't hear a word Grandma was saying.

". . . I will always love you. Please believe that. People are going to tell you a lot of things about me. They'll say I'm crazy, I'm mean, that I've been a horrible mother. Don't believe them. I love you. I will always love you. What happened between your father and me has nothing to do with how I feel about you. It wasn't your fault. You'll always be mine no matter where I go . . ."

Later, Dad knocked on my door.

"Eddie?"

"Yeah?"

"Open the door. I want to talk to you."

I unlocked it and sat down on my bed.

He walked in and stood over me.

"What's this I hear about you disrespecting Grandma?"

"She talked bad about Ma. I hate her."

"Eddie . . ."

"I hate this house. I hate this street."

"Don't say that."

"Grandma's mean. I hate her."

"I don't ever want to hear those words come out of your mouth again about your grandmother. Do you understand me? I said, do you understand me?"

"Yes," I mumbled.

"Now she has her opinions, but she's still your grand-mother and you have to show her respect."

"What about the dogs, Dad? You're not gonna listen to her about the dogs are you?"

"There's no way around it. They have to go."

"WHAT?"

"I'm sorry, Eddie."

"You're sorry. Ma's sorry. Everybody's sorry."

"Look, son"—he sat on the bed next to me—"I know all this has been hard on you, your mother leaving and . . ." He swallowed hard and bit his bottom lip. "But it's hard on me too. She left both of us, buddy."

"But *you* let her go, Dad. You let her walk away."

"It's not that simple, Eddie. It's complicated."

"Did you hurt her?"

"No. I don't think so. Maybe."

"Do you love her?"

"Well, yes, of course I love her, but . . ."

"Then make her come back, Dad. Bring her back."

"I can't. She won't. It's hard to explain. When you get older, Eddie, it'll be easier for you to understand."

"So that's it? When I get older?"

"Son . . ."

He tried to put his arm around my shoulder, but I wouldn't let him.

"Stop crying, son. For God'ssake. Listen. Maybe you need some time to yourself."

I didn't answer.

He got up, looking like someone had kicked him in his gut, and left.

I was glad because I couldn't stand to look at him anymore. The dogs, Ma, Grandma. I couldn't believe any of it was happening. I turned the tape back on.

". . . Try to remember all the good times. Remember all the special moments . . ."

I started thinking about the last thing me and Ma had done together. We went to this beach that looked like something out of a TV movie. The sand was all white. When you put your feet in it, it felt like someone was under there giving you a massage or something. Really. That's how nice it was. The water was blue and you could see your hands in it.

I didn't expect to be there, because it was a school day and Ma didn't tell me anything about the beach that morning when she was putting my peanut butter and jelly sandwich in my lunchbox. So when they called my name over the loud-speaker and said I was supposed to report to the main office, I thought I was in trouble, especially when I saw Ma walking back and forth outside of the office with this upset expression on her face. That was it. When they called your parents in, it was all over. Only, Ma was gorgeous. Her skin looked golden and her hair was combed just right and she had these big, pretty silver earrings on that I had never seen before. She was wearing these jeans and a red blouse that showed her beautiful figure. I guess she's average height, but this day she looked like a giant goddess.

All I could do was look up at her.

"Hi, baby." She smiled, all excited like a little girl. "Let's go."

"But . . ."

"Where's your books and things? Didn't they tell you?"

"Huh?"

"I'm taking you out early today. You remember that ap-pointment you have." She winked at me. Then in a low voice, "We're going to spend some time together. Just you and me."

And that's how we ended up on this beach. I kept feeling

like something was wrong, but I didn't know what. Ma kept looking at me like she wanted to say something real important, only she'd never say it. Once I caught her looking at me like I wasn't her son or something, like she was looking at me for the first time. It was spooky.

"Ma, are you alright?"

It took her a while to answer, but then she said, "Huh? What's the matter, son?"

I figured she was embarrassed, so I let it go.

"Nothing."

Then she kind of looked out at the water like I wasn't even there, like I was in a tiny white lifeboat drifting far, far away from the shore. And she grabbed my hand, held it real tight, like she didn't want to let go.

". . . When you remember all the special times, you'll feel how much I love you. Someday, when you're old enough, you'll understand why people who love each other sometimes leave each other.

"Your father, he's a good man. We just don't belong together anymore. Something happened. Maybe I'm the one who's different. I'm not sure. It's like I've died inside this house and nobody knows it but me.

"I want to take you with me. You're a child. It would be selfish. You need a home. So I have to leave you, only for a little while, much as I don't want to.

"Eddie, I don't know how much of this is making sense to you, but I had to try to explain. The only regret I . . . besides having to leave you, . . . I couldn't find the words. I wanted to explain this to you before I left. Wanted to hold you. Wish I could be there now to hold you when I know how much you're hurting . . . I'm sorry, Eddie. I'm so sorry . . . I'm hurting . . . too . . . Have to go. I love you very, very much. You'll hear from me again soon."

So that's why I made my decision. Now, this morning, me and Malcolm are running away, just like Ma did. We're going to be with her. She wrote me a few letters, so I know where she lives. The three of us are going to live together. I didn't even tell her. I didn't tell anybody, except Malcolm. I want to surprise her. Ma will understand, about the dogs and everything else.

I'm never coming back.

We found her, but everything just seems to keep getting worse and worse. First of all, this place where she lives has garbage in front of it and the hallways smell like pee. Some big, ugly guy answered her door and he wasn't too happy to see us. I asked Ma who he was, but I guess she was so excited when she heard my voice that she didn't hear my question.

She doesn't look too good. Her face looks older than the last time I saw her and she's lost a lot of weight. But it felt real good when she hugged me and that's why I thought everything was gonna be alright. I told her about us moving and Liz and the new house and the dogs and how we ran away to be with her and all.

But now that she's in the kitchen, and I'm sitting on her bed, in her room, which is smaller than mine and has no windows, everything just feels strange again. Malcolm found one of her socks and carried it in his mouth to a corner and fell asleep. I just look at the beat-up floor with the tiles that don't match, and her little bed, and the one chair, but I don't want to hurt her feelings, so I don't say anything about her new place.

I feel so weird inside, like one of those guys in a horror movie who knows something bad's about to happen to him, but he doesn't know what.

"I'm so glad to see you, Eddie," she says coming back into the room and giving me a kiss on my forehead. She kneels in front of me and holds my hands. "Now, you know I had to call your father. He'll be here soon to pick you up."

"What are you talking about?" I am looking at her pink bathrobe because if I look straight at her, I know I will start crying again. "I thought we were going to be together now."

"Oh, Eddie." She closes her eyes. For a long moment, the

room fills up with the loudest quiet I've ever heard. Ma sits next to me on the bed. "I know how you feel about the dogs. Especially Malcolm. But there's some things you can't do anything about. 'Cept figure out how you're going to get through them."

I know this is not happening. Ma's not telling me this. I close my eyes, but I still hear her voice.

"Listen to me, Eddie. Do you know that the hardest thing I ever had to do in my whole life was walk past your room the night I left? I thought so many times about turning around and coming back to get you. I wake up crying. I wonder if leaving was worth it. Sometimes I even think about what it would be like to have you here with me." She squeezes my hand quickly, then stops.

"That's what I've been thinking too, Ma!"

"I couldn't. Look at this place."

"I don't care," I say, "as long as I'm with you."

"Your father can give you a better life."

"Yeah. He's doing a great job so far."

"Give him a chance." I turn away from her. "Things will get better."

"I don't care. It doesn't matter. I want to be with you. Don't you love Dad? Even a little bit?"

Now I'm crying. I wipe my eyes with my shirtsleeve.

"Yes."

"Then . . . I don't get it." I turn around. "Just come back, Ma, and things can be the way they used to be. First we'll get rid of Liz and then they won't have to get rid of the dogs and then Grandma can go back home and we can move back into our old house and—" But that sad look in her eyes makes me stop. It's like the way you look when you feel sorry for someone. Like I've got some horrible disease and there's nothing she can do to save me. I can't take it. So I turn away from her again.

Ma puts her hands on my shoulders and turns me gently around. I still won't look at her. "Do you believe that I love *you*?" she asks me.

"If you loved me, you'd let me stay with you or . . . or you'd come back with me," I mumble to my sneakers. "If you loved me"—I face her—"you never would have left me."

She lets out a big sigh, and looks right at me. I know she wants to cry. But I can't help it. I have to keep talking.

"Ma, why didn't you tell me? You just walked away like it was nothing. Like *I* was nothing."

"I'm so sorry, baby."

"I needed you, Ma. And you left me."

"Honey." Her eyes are about to spill over. "I should have told you."

"You left me," I keep saying.

"I'm sorry, Eddie. I was wrong not to tell you. I'm sorry. I'm sorry. Please. Forgive me."

At first I don't say anything. My head is down. Ma gently lifts my chin. I can see her tears starting to go down her cheeks. "Please. Ma. Don't cry. Ma. I forgive you."

Now we are both crying. We are holding each other like we are both each other's baby. Here's the weird thing: this time, all the crying feels good.

It's Sunday. I'm back with Dad. I'm still not happy about being here. Ma said I can call her anytime I want, and when she gets a new place, I'll be able to stay with her for a few days sometimes. Dad was mad about me running away, but he talked real soft to me about the whole thing just once and that was it.

I'm at the lake. I woke up early this morning to say good-bye to Malcolm and Caesar. Dad took them away to a shelter. I try not to think about it because I know he made a mistake.

I still have Malcolm's old leash in my hand. I don't want to let it go but finally I leave it on a rock near the edge of the water and start throwing pebbles at it, until little by little, it slides into the lake. One thing makes me smile. It's this funny light that catches the last link of Malcolm's chain and makes it shine real bright before it disappears into the blue.

The Ride

Frank got into the cab. He had no time to look at the driver's face.

"Logan Airport," he said.

Dammit. His Rolex had just decided to stop working. Wasn't there a clock somewhere in this damn car? And what was that god-awful smell?

He tapped his manicured nails on the face of his watch four quick times, then held the round glass to his ear. "What are you waiting for?" he asked the back of the gray and black head he saw in front of him.

No answer.

"Hey, buddy. I got a plane to catch," Frank said, pulling at his tie and leaning forward.

"Logan," the cabbie said, turning off the engine. "Any luggage?"

"Yes. My suit . . ."

"Those?" The cabbie casually pointed at the two leather bags on the curb.

"Yes. Those."

"Uh-huh."

Frank was starting to sweat in the summer morning heat. "Well?" he asked.

"Well what?" the back of the head said.

Oh, Frank thought. *One of those lazy ones. The type who makes his kind look bad. Not a drop of ambition.* "You're supposed to put my bags in the car."

The driver turned around. His face was hard, dark amber. "I'm not *supposed* to do anything."

Oh boy. "Look . . ."

"No. You look. I'm going to open the trunk for you. Get your shit and put it in. If you need help, I'll help you."

Frank sat there for a moment, completely unsure of what to do next.

The driver got out of the car and unlocked the trunk. He walked back around to the passenger side. "Let's go," he said. "You got a plane to catch or what?" He opened the front door and sat back down.

Frank gripped the backseat door handle as if he could crush it between his fingers, then pushed the door open. *Smart-ass,* he thought. *Okay. I'll put the bags in the trunk. Fuck this black bastard. We get to the airport, he's finished. One phone call.*

The driver watched Frank struggle with the suitcases. He watched him through his rearview mirror put the bags in the trunk and slam it shut.

Frank got back in the car. "I'm behind schedule," he said.

The driver started the engine. "What time is your flight?"

"Ten-fifteen. I need you to get moving."

"I need you to relax. What airline? You want the business shuttle?"

"Yes. US Air, near the—"

"I know the drill, champ. Now, in order for me to do my job and get you where you want to be on time, you're gonna have to give up that control. You got my cab stinkin' with tension."

"What?"

"I can't concentrate on what I'm doin' if I'm all locked up in your shit, ya dig? I been doin' this for thirty-five years. You don't like what I'm sayin', you can call another cab. I can take your bags out and you can start your morning all over again."

Frank couldn't believe what he was hearing. No one talked to him like this, least of all a fucking cab driver. He'd have to remember all this for later. This clown had no clue who he was dealing with. He rubbed one of the twenty-four-carat gold and diamond cufflinks he'd bought last week. Then he wiped his forehead.

"Whatcha gonna do, my man?" the driver asked, smiling and leaning back on his elbow.

"Let's go," Frank growled.

"Alright." He pulled away from the curb into traffic. "Remember what I said. I need you to be cool. No matter what."

No matter what. He is five years old. There are red marks on his arms and legs where his mother has scrubbed him clean. "No matter what, Frank. You don't play with those boys," she is saying. She'd snatched him out of the sandbox as soon as she realized he was playing with that Black boy. They were holding hands.

He'd cried and cried. "Wanna play! Wanna play!"

"No, Frank. Mommy said, 'No.' "

Frank is fourteen. He is with his older brother, Sammy, 16. They are sweating, playing basketball in the park. Sammy's naked chest reflects the shadow lines of the metal fence, as he makes the time-out sign and walks toward him.

"C'mere," Sammy says, gesturing to him.

"What I do?" Frank asks.

"Nothin'. C'mere, Frankie."

"Okay. Okay."

They huddle in the center of the court. "Lissen-a-me. You listenin', Frankie?"

"Yeah. What?"

Sammy lowers his voice and looks over at the Black guys standing at the other end, waiting. "No matter what happens. Even if these niggers beat us, we're still betta. Y'hear what I'm sayin'? We're still betta 'cause we're white. Y'understand, Frankie?"

He didn't really. But he never forgot. For as long as he

could remember, it had been him against them. He lived in his world. They lived in theirs.

"Shit!" the driver said. He pulled over and turned the motor off. They were in the middle of a poor, Black section of the city.

"What's going on? What's happening?" Frank asked, trying to stay calm.

"My man. Here's the deal. Take your tie off and all that jewelry."

"Why? What do you want? What's going to happen?"

"Nothing, if you do what I tell you. Roll up your sleeves, put that stuff in your pockets, get out of the car, and be cool," the driver said, and left the front seat.

The punk in Frank was starting to get hysterical. He couldn't move. He didn't know whether to stay in the car or take his chances in the street. *Can't let them see me scared,* he thought. *I can run if I have to.*

He decided to get out of the car. He stepped out and looked around. His heart had fallen out of his chest and dropped into his stomach. His shirt stuck to his back like plastic wrap. Frank didn't see the cab driver anywhere.

"Flat," the cabbie said, popping up from the right front side of the car. "I'ma need your help."

Frank looked like he was going to pass out.

"What's your name, man?" the cabbie asked, frowning.

"Frank."

"Bend down here next to this tire with me. That's it. Frank, you got to relax, man. You're stiff. This is a rough corner. I need you loose, Frank, so we can get through this. Right now you got 'victim' written all over you. You're gonna pull yourself together and be my eyes. Tell me what you see across the street there."

"Guys standing around. They're talking, I guess. Not doing anything."

"Good. I'm going to go to the trunk and get what we need." He stood up, looked around quickly, missing nothing, drenching himself in the energy. He opened the trunk, grabbed the spare, the jack, and the tire iron. The driver rolled the spare to Frank. "Now you and I are going to change this tire and have us a conversation. What you wanna talk about?"

"I don't know." Frank laid his jacket on the hood of the car. "Anything."

"Keep going."

"Celtics. Sox. What do you want to talk about?"

The driver jacked the car up slowly. "How 'bout we talk about power?"

"Okay." Frank pried the hubcap off. It hit the pavement with a metallic clatter.

They took turns loosening the bolts.

"Make a lot of money, don't you, Frank? Young guy like you. What are you, twenty-seven, twenty-eight?"

"Twenty-eight."

"Like makin' that money, huh?"

Frank gave a small smile. "Yeah. I like it."

"Make you feel powerful?"

"You could say that."

"Let me let you in on a little secret. Gangsta-thinkin' dudes can't wait to spank a sucker like you. They just wanna smack you 'side your head for the hell of it. And you can't understand that, can you?"

"No. Well, maybe."

"You a walkin' contradiction. Got all that money and you're uptight. That don't make no kinda sense."

The flat was off. Frank looked through the space beneath the car. He could see the sidewalk where the Black men were hanging out. A pair of long legs were moving in their direction. This guy had to be tall. He was taking his time, but he was definitely coming toward them.

"One of those guys. He's coming this way."

Remaining in a crouched position, Frank made his way to the front of the car to get a better look. Not only was this guy tall, he was big. He was wearing a black hood and a baggy pair of black jeans.

"Keep talking. Help me with the spare," the driver said.

"What are we going to do?" Frank whispered, moving back to the driver.

"I'm cool. Where's your power, Frank?" The driver stood up to face the man walking toward them. "Mornin'," he said.

Frank's hands were moving faster, pushing the tire iron, tightening the bolts.

The stranger was smiling. "Good morning." He looked down at Frank. "Y'all need a hand?"

The driver guessed that the stranger was young, probably no more than nineteen or twenty. "We cool, man. 'Preciate you askin'."

"Aw-ight," he began, walking away. "I be over there you need anything."

"Thanks, brother," the driver said. Bending down next to Frank, he said, "That's power. Steppin' into what you don't know with no fear. Being able to walk away at any time. I could do that right now, you know. Just walk away. What about you?"

"You mean right now?"

"I mean your j-o-b. Can you step off whenever you want?"

The driver double-checked each bolt. Then Frank began to lower the car back down to the ground. "People depend on me," he said." I got investments. Other things. No. I can't just walk."

"They got you by your balls, man. I ain't got your money. But I sure as hell got me."

Frank rubbed the back of his neck. "Done," he said, brushing himself off. "Are we going to make it?"

"We're only five minutes away now."

"Oh." He walked back to his side of the cab. "I've never been this way before."

"I know."

They got back in the car and were on their way. The air in the cab had changed. It was clearer, easier to breathe.

Frank leaned closer to the driver. He heard him humming along to a jazz standard on the radio.

He remembered the music at the office Christmas party years ago. Frank was twenty-one then, straight out of Advanced Business Management II. His first big job. She was Black, exotic, real pretty, did something or other in the office. He'd heard that Black girls were good lovers. Never went out with one before. Wasn't sure he wanted to, but boy, did she excite him. Caramel legs dripping into patent leather pumps. He *had* to ask her to dance. Everyone was drunk by then. No one would bother him about it.

She put her hands on his shoulders. Her perfume tiptoed up his nostrils and he almost lost it. Somehow he made it through the dance. When it was over, he asked her to walk with him outside. He thought they could sit in his car so maybe they could talk. If that was alright with her. They sat awkwardly for a few minutes, finding conversation—how cold it was, when it would snow, the dark flavor of the sky, the heat coming from the vents, his hand touching her thigh, the taste of her lips, her hard, brown nipple rolling against the sweat of his palm.

He never saw her again. Never even asked what her name was. Didn't matter. Wasn't even curious. He'd stolen a chocolate chip cookie from an empty cookie jar.

"Listen," Frank said to the cabbie, "you know my name. What's yours?"

"Friends call me 'Andrew.' "

"Andrew," he repeated, as if learning the word for the first time. "Any kids?"

"Three. Two boys and one girl. All growed up. On their own. You?"

"Naw. Not yet. One day. When I find the right woman."

"Well," Andrew said, pulling to the curb, "we're here. Just enough time for you to make it."

Frank sat there for a second, not wanting to leave. He knew corporate would take care of the tip, but he reached inside his pocket and grabbed what cash he could. He put it in Andrew's hand and let his own hand linger there against Andrew's brown-lined palm. "This has been the most interesting ride I've ever had, Andrew," he said.

Andrew chuckled. "We had us some moments, didn't we? You take care, man. And remember, be cool."

"I will."

Frank held on to the door handle, then opened the door.

Professor

The map is not the territory.

—ALFRED KORSBYBSKI

Slowly, they filled The Great Hall. The night was cold. The music was low, soothing. The lights were blue. They had come to hear Brother Z. He was making a special appearance in the States on his way to Nigeria, where he was also a featured speaker.

These days, magazines flashed his face times ten. His eyes hit you first, then the subtle curl of his lips that said, *You know I'm right.* Most white people spit his name out, the syllables getting stuck between their teeth. Black folks held the sound of him inside, their tongues gently releasing, one at a time, each of his letters. He was the media's favorite target, and Black folks' just plain favorite.

Most of the "cultural people" sat together in the Hall, with their long garments, cornrows, dreads, and Kente cloth. Every now and then, they gave "The Professor" in the front row near the stage a disdainful look. He alternately jumped up, then fell back down into his chair according to the potency of the swallow from his Wild Irish Rose. He had come early to make sure he got a good seat.

Brah Z was bad y'understan'?

In his younger days, Prof was a straight-backed, earth-brown man with a proud walk. Everyone called him "Top Shelf" for his style of dressing and his way with the ladies. He was a bent-over-walking man now with a silvery, three-day beard. All of the guys in the old gang from the neighborhood were in graveyards or prisons. On his way to the Hall, he'd poured them a libation, a few drops on the ground, in the tradition.

His two favorite pastimes were drinking and watching. Called himself a "behaviorist." Loved to study folk. Up close or from a distance, didn't matter. The human condition. Loved watchin' it go by.

Poly-sci majors had descended on the crowd. Black boots. Tight lips. Jeans. Malcolm pendants. Mandela buttons. Army fatigues. And a copy of the most politically correct book ever written that we all should read and memorize.

The poets floated in and out of consciousness, depending on how deep they thought they were.

And everyone waited for Brother Z.

Chaka, The Heaviest Poet In Chicago (that's what his business card said), had taken the red-eye out of O'Hare to be there. He never brought a woman to these things. She'd be too much trouble after he stepped down from the stage, when all the sisters came around to touch him with a smile, let the fragrance of their oils kiss his lips, taste the scent of his Blackness.

As Chaka ascended the steps to the podium, he searched his pockets for "Onyx Pearl," the poem he'd scribbled down on a grease-spotted napkin on the plane. He'd tease them first, then take them to the bridge.

Shrouded in blue, he began:

onyx pearl
Afri
ca

"Yeah!" somebody yelled.

mother
onyx
woman
smooth
curved
fitting just right in
the night of my
despair
splitting daylight in half
i am
surrounded by your softness

The brothers squirmed and moaned.

take me

The sisters closed their eyes.

your son in need
of your embrace
lead me
like a fish in water
to your secret space
give me
your pain

"Yes!" someone shouted. Only Prof remained unmoved, and managed a spitty "That ain't Brah Z" before he was shushed on the downstroke back into his seat.

give me
your pain
give me
your pain
and
lead me
I am
your
Black man.

Sisters hummed and smiled. Brothers beamed, thrusting out their chests, as they surveyed the crowd.

When Chaka finished his third poem, the sisters were

flushed. The brothers were shifting in their seats. There was a bulge in Chaka's pants as he gathered his papers amid applause and hurried backstage.

"He's coming!" someone screamed.

A row of kufis tilted. The lights grew dim. Then, whispers wrapped in darkness.

Brother Z was dressed in black from head to toe. The only part of him that shone beneath the light was his handsome walnut face. His bodyguards barely visible, he loomed in the darkness. Their angel of Blackness.

Prof breathed in the vision. He wanted to remember everything.

The crowd was eager. They loved Brother Z. Every inch. He knew exactly what they wanted, what they needed.

"My beautiful Afrikan brothers and sisters . . ."

Sweetly, warmly, he gave it to them.

". . . Nubian nurturers . . . pyramid planners . . ."

Gentle wisdom of ancient truths he used to part their lips. With loving politics, he held them close, eye to eye, and stroked the essence of their core.

". . . strutting not shackled, building not beaten . . ."

He felt their spirits flow beneath his touch, surrender to the urging of his passion. He had a gift.

"Can we, brothers and sisters? Can we *love* one another?"

He let them touch him back. Arouse awareness even higher, 'til neither one could stop.

"Well!"

They begged for every drop of what they knew he had to give.

"Bra-tha Z!"

"Teach!"

Their signals led him to his mark.

"Yes!"

His temples pulsed. He strained and pushed and they were with him. The Great Hall grew heated. Hearts beat faster. Shimmers warmed the crowd. Brother Z was in them now. He was floating, swimming deep in their subconscious, touching primal nerves, plunging depths. He and they were one.

". . . watery miles, oceans of blood, deities disguised, flesh of our flesh sold, once-a-year-new clothes, one good foot left to run away with—*our seed survived*. For us to *die*? Our ancestors watch. For us to die? From sky to heart, they pull. Old ones press their lips against the wind, send a message through the breeze: *Slay plantation. Lay foundation. Soar above survive—and thrive!*"

They embraced him as he filled the center of their being and vibrated through their very souls. Prof nearly passed out.

No one moved when it was over. They let the feeling

linger. By the time the clapping broke the spell, Brother Z had disappeared.

Slowly, The Great Hall emptied. The air was thick with human odor and exalted conversation.

Prof stumbled half contentedly out into the night. It didn't matter now that everyone else had written him off. All these so-Black people who would change the world. Brother Z had spoken. To *him*. Included him. Reminded him of who he once was and still could be.

He had to regroup. The Brother always touched his vulnerability. Took the dreamy from his bottle. Changed his liquor into bile. Made him feel his black nakedness in the open sea, forcing him to remember how far he'd gone, was still going, from the shore. The Brother woke him up, in the middle of his sleep, in the middle of the ocean, choking on the salt water, slicing with his arms and legs, looking back at all those teeth he was still outswimming, at least for now.

He headed for the large outcropping of rock a few feet from the entrance. Twice he nearly fell climbing to the top. As he sat down, the dark cold melted into the seat of his pants, seeping beneath the surface of his skin, chilling his buttocks and thighs. He sat, nonetheless, listening to the night sounds of the people, watching the ghosts of steam briefly hover then disappear above them. He saw hats, sleeves, gloves couple, uncouple in the doorway, the people forming random circles, triangles, squares, rectangles connecting, dissolving. It reminded Prof of an aerial shot from a Busby Berkeley movie he'd seen as a kid. He watched the people and wondered when they had closed him out. When they had decided he was no longer a brother.

He looked down at his dry, wrinkled hand, then took a good swallow from his bottle. Funny how the only thing changing was him. He looked closely at the crowd for any differences Brother Z had made—a ragged pulse, a rhythm off its beat, some brave, new color, just one body moving in ways it never moved before. But there was nothing unfamiliar. He'd seen all this before. This energy. These people. Even the faces never really changed. There was the hungry one who'd been shut down as a child, the patient one who covered her bruises with veils of smiles, the tough one threatened by any pair of eyes he couldn't widen with fear. Everyone seemed to know exactly how to stand and what to say.

For Prof, it was different. He had come to be awakened. Brother Z took him out of his element. These folks, they seemed like they were back in theirs. They had come to make sure they had not missed a beat. They wanted affirmation, needed absolution, longed to be locked into who they were, righteously steeled. Nothing could touch them now.

Prof wrapped his lips around the bottle's neck and cornered the last drop. He stood the bottle up next to him on the rocks, a fragile, transparent monument to the night. He looked up and saw the same moon that had followed him there, waiting to take him home. He stepped down, one unsure foot at a time. Prof walked away from The Great Hall, his eyes following the moonlight as it lit his path down the same streets he always walked. A few blocks later, he collapsed into the fuzzy sleep he knew so well, in his favorite spot, next to the corner bus stop.

Sunday Visit

The old one and the young one stood in line with the others. The little girl, Elaina, looked up at the high metal fence with its razor-barbed coils that cut the air and stretched around the grassy spaces, trees and buildings inside it. She shivered. Her hair was all pigtails covered with plastic bursts of red, yellow, and purple. Her nose could smell a jellybean twenty miles away, and when she stood way up, high on her tippy toes, she could reach the top of the silver man's hat on Grampy's belt buckle.

Elaina was wearing her new dress. It was a misty violet, like the tiny flowers that grew in the front yard across the street where she lived. She felt itchy and uncomfortable. Elaina could hardly wait to see her mother.

"Child, what's wrong with you?" Grammy was saying. "You 'bout to squeeze the life out my fingers. And stop that poutin'. Put on a pretty face for your mama. You act like you never been to this here prison before."

It was a gray day. Easter Sunday.

They were standing next to a tall, glass tower. Elaina's eyes followed it from the bottom up as it rose like a giant fist through the sky. The man up there controlled this world. He sat in the clouds and decided who would move, who would stop, who would live, who would die. If a rabbit bounded across the field, he saw it. When a robin flew from one branch to another, he watched its flight. And if an inmate was moving toward the outside of the gate, he made sure she stopped moving forever. With loaded rifle he stood now, looking through the glass, watching the people below. He pressed a button. The gate opened.

The crowd pushed their way past Grammy and Elaina. Elaina was too frightened to move. She knew what was coming next. Maybe if she stood still and imagined her mother's face, she could magically be inside already, talking with her and holding her hand.

A tall female guard was on post, standing at the doorway, smiling.

"Just look at her, Mary"—she motioned to the too-much-purple-lipstick guard at the desk—"a little lady."

Elaina didn't trust them. They wore dark uniforms with something that shined like jewelry pinned to their chests. They winked, unlocked doors, and put their bored faces in hers to see what part of her looked like her mother. They'd shake their heads, feeling sorry for her. Shame. Crying shame a beautiful little girl like her got to have a mother like that. Then they used that machine.

It was long, shaped like the chain saw Grampy had in his shed behind the house. It was sneaky and it screamed when it came close.

A third guard, who was big as a bear, had the machine in her hand. She was moving toward Elaina. "Now hold still, honey. Y'hear me?" she said. Elaina began to cry. "I'm not going to hurt you."

She cried even louder, balling up her fists and closing her eyes.

"Poor thing. She's 'fraid a the machine," the desk guard said.

As Elaina looked up, it was coming at her. It was squealing, excited. She closed her eyes again. Felt it whir down her back and across her tiny buttocks. If she could pretend, like Mommy told her, that it was a magic wand that made every part of her brave, it couldn't hurt her. It couldn't frighten her. But then, she felt it buzzing up and down her legs. Then back up to her shoulders. Now it was buzzing loudly, close to her neck. She began to tremble and the tears started again. It was still buzzing all over the front of her dress now, like some slow and painful haircut she didn't ask for in places where haircuts weren't supposed to happen.

Finally, it stopped. She was safe.

"I wanna see Mommy," she said, wiping her eyes.

"What you got in your hand, baby?" the guard who had searched her asked.

"Nothing."

The guard tried to gently pry Elaina's fingers open. Elaina held tight.

"Open up your hand for the nice lady, sweetie," Grammy whispered, embarrassed.

"I don't want to. It's for Mommy. I don't want to."

"Elaina!"

The guard looked through the spaces of her little fingers and saw a crumpled, yellow flower. "Oh no, baby," she said. "You can't bring that in."

"It's for Mommy."

"Sorry, sugah. But you have to leave it here. Mommy's not allowed to have it."

"You have to do what the lady says or you can't see Mommy," Grammy said, losing patience.

She had left all her belongings in the car, including her white, church Bible, figuring that if the word of God couldn't get in, simply wasn't no use tryin' to bring in nothin' else. She'd given up fighting with these people long ago over anything that made sense. If she'd only known what her granddaughter had intended on doing, she would have put an end to it right after the church service. All this nonsense over one little flower.

Grammy put her hand out. "Give it to me."

Elaina lowered her head and stood there.

She heard that voice Grammy used when she didn't care how many people were around. That voice that told her she would spank her right here, right now. "Young lady, if you don't bring me that flower right now, I'll really give you something to cry about."

She handed the flower to her grandmother.

Grammy handed it to the guard.

In exchange, the guard gave Elaina that same old smile she always gave her. "I'll just keep it here for you 'til you get back," she said, winking. "Okay, darlin'?"

Elaina turned away, pouting hard, and grabbed Grammy's hand as they walked through the doors of the visiting room. She thought the walls were booger green. No color, no posters like in her bedroom. A sad little room that always felt empty, even when it was full. There were a lot of signs about do this and don't do that. Old ripped signs with tape that didn't stick anymore and faded words. And new signs too, every time they came.

Elaina raced to the table that Mommy liked to sit at, next to the soda machine. It was the last table left. There were all kinds of people there. Big people. Little people. White. Black. Spanish. Men with women. Women with women. She couldn't help watching everything. She could never tell the difference between the visitors and the inmates.

"Stop staring, Elaina," Grammy scolded.

From someplace behind her eyes, Grammy watched the people, never where they could see her looking. There were other little girls and boys in their Easter suits and dresses, with their parents and grandparents, sitting in the hard plastic orange seats at the wooden tables. Their short legs were hanging off the ends of the chairs, their feet kicking at the metal supports. Some of the children were only babies. They had been bundled up by one family member or another to wonder at Mommy's face, remember her voice, her smell, and feel her necessary touch. The mothers all seemed to hold their babies the same way—as if they were glass dolls in danger of shattering into a jagged pile on the floor.

Grammy looked at her granddaughter and remembered when her daughter, Freeda, had been her little girl. Those days when she'd pick her up just to rub her nose against her skin, blow ripples of giggles into her belly button, put her tiny hand on hers, palm to palm. The moments Freeda had made her laugh, up in church that time, her little fingers grabbing the back of the pew in front of them. The sudden hum of laughter politely coughed into the tissues and white-gloved fists behind her during "Onward, Christian Soldiers," as the congregation stared at Freeda's naked bottom instead of the hymn book.

Those times seemed so far away now. The way Mrs. Sarah Ann Johnson explained it to herself was that ever since the arrest, there had been a film around her daughter. An invisible, resistant film she'd given up trying to break through. She first saw it at the hearing, when Freeda was in handcuffs. Something different about her. Something changed. Or was it something that had always been there and no longer had a

94

place to hide? She could smell the jail on her as they rode home. Freeda had been silent. The film had begun to harden then, and it just kept getting thicker.

Visit by visit, she saw it become part of Freeda's body. The way she spoke. The way she walked. This wasn't her child. But there were glimpses. Freeda would reach out, become her baby again, only to pull back when she looked deep into her mother and saw that she was not forgiven, maybe never could be, for what had happened.

Hard to believe it had been two years now. Mrs. Johnson began to tap her bright red, pointy nails on the table. She looked at the big clock on the wall, then over to the door that the inmates entered from, then back to the clock. She wondered if something had gone wrong. Maybe Freeda had done something and they'd taken her visiting privileges away. No one ever tells you anything in this place.

Elaina looked around at the other children talking to their mommies. Why was her mommy taking so long?

The door opened slightly, then closed. Ten minutes later, it opened again.

"I see her! Mommy's coming! Mommy's coming!"

Freeda walked through the door. She was tall and elegant, even in a pair of jeans. Today, she had dressed up in her best skirt and blouse. She felt sick inside. This was one of those days that scared her because she had no fear. Today she welcomed the easy, peaceful arms of death. But when she saw Elaina, she giggled. Freeda had given up a lot of what free folks called "conveniences" (here they were necessities) and she'd called in just as many favors to pay for Elaina's dress. She knew it was worth all she'd been through when she saw her daughter wearing it.

It was that sweet-and-sour feeling again, no place she could locate, but everywhere inside her. It lifted her for a moment. By making her daughter happy, she could be visible in Elaina's world, live outside these walls, if only for a minute. It sunk her just as quickly as she realized how much of a ghost she'd already become.

Elaina couldn't wait any longer. She jumped out of her chair and grabbed her mother by the waist, hugging her and pulling at her arm for her to bend down and give her a kiss.

"You know the rules, Freeda," the guard at the desk up front said.

The inmates were all staring at her. She'd gotten used to that. *Baby Killer.* That's what the TV and newspapers had called her. The words still choking her when she tried to talk to someone about her charge, turning her into a loner, keeping her finally, more simply, to herself.

"Sugar plum"—she squatted down, straightening Elaina's dress—"go sit down with Grammy. I have to give the guard a piece of paper, and I'll be right back."

Freeda held her head up, and with her long legs, she crossed the room to the desk. She walked back over to the table where her daughter and mother were, and she picked Elaina up and tickled her face with kisses on her nose, kisses on her eyes, kisses on her forehead. Her eyes were wet when she put her down and went around to the other side of the table to hug her mother. Mrs. Johnson's body was rigid as Freeda hugged her tightly. She turned her head so Freeda could kiss her on the cheek.

"Mommy! Look at my dress!"

Freeda sat at the table. She pretended to look around. "Who is this gorgeous girl at my table wearing such a pretty dress? Excuse me, little girl, do you know where my sugar plum went?"

Elaina started to laugh.

"It's me, Mommy."

"Oh! It is you. Laney! You're the pretty girl in the pretty dress! C'mere. Come sit on Mommy's lap. Let me hold you."

Freeda's hair was dark brown, cut close to her milk chocolate face. Her fingers were long, slender. Her nails were perfect. She stroked Elaina's hair. "How you feel today, Mama?" Freeda asked.

"Not bad."

"Arthritis bothering you?"

"Only at night."

97

"I'm so glad you could come." Then it all seeped out. "I'm not doing too good. I don't know if I'm gonna make it."

"Nonsense. Course you gonna make it. You have to make it."

"I thought you weren't coming when they didn't call me."

"Your sugar plum was busy causin' a scene with them guards. She wanted to bring you some old yellow flower she had."

"Did she?" Freeda smiled down at Elaina and kissed her forehead. "They get nuts about stuff like that. Everything's a drug or a weapon. Contraband. They got nothin' else to do."

"Wouldna been in here in the first place if you'd stayed away from them drugs."

Elaina was trying to get down so she could get Mommy's cigarettes from the machine.

"Please, Mama. Not today. I can't handle it today. Sit still, Laney."

"You wouldn't listen. Had to move in with that bum. He wudn't worth two nickels. Keepin' you smokin' them reefers all the time."

"Mama."

"Mommy, can I get your cigarettes?"

"If you hadn'ta been smokin' them reefers, my granbaby would be alive today. Praise God." Freeda's mother covered her face. "He was just a baby."

Conscious of the guard up front, Freeda shifted Elaina in her lap and softly tapped the floor with her foot.

"Mommy!"

"Mama, it was an accident. I loved Nathaniel."

"Mommy!"

"Wait a minute, Laney. Grammy has to do it. You can help."

"Here." Mrs. Johnson felt inside her pockets and brought out a handful of machine tokens. Elaina grabbed a few and headed for the machine. Mrs. Johnson stood up to walk with Elaina. "Bought you tokens like I always do."

Freeda wanted to scream, but she'd learned how to freeze what she wanted to do what she had to. When they returned to the table, her mother placed a pack of cigarettes, matches, and a plastic bottle of Coke in front of her. Freeda spoke in a low tone.

"Thanks." She waited 'til her mother was seated. "How many times do I have to say I'm sorry?"

"Won't bring Nathaniel back."

"Nothing will bring Nathaniel back." Freeda placed her hand on her forehead, then looked into her mother's eyes. "He was *my* son, Mama. I have to live with it. Every day I sit in here. It's all I ever think about. I've gone over it in my head a million times. I think about it so much sometimes I think I'm going crazy. Can't even sleep without dreaming about it."

Summertime. Big blue sky. Nathaniel. Something gnawing at Freeda as she gave her items to the super-market cashier.

"C'mon, Laney."

She grabbed her daughter's hand.

"We have to get back to the house."

"Buy me some cookies, Mommy."

"Not now, Laney. We gotta go."

Gnawing. Pointed teeth nibbling.

She'd finally gotten little Nathaniel to sleep. He'd been crying for at least two hours, nonstop. Just her luck to have a colicky one second time around. She'd run out of everything—diapers, formula, cigarettes, patience. She felt like her skull had been cracked on the left side of her forehead, above her eye.

It was only supposed to be for a minute. One minute. A quick trip to the corner store and back because there was no one to watch the baby. She thought a little bit of fresh air might even do her some good. Clear her head. Confuse her aching. Make her forget the only break she'd had in three days was a series of broken lines of restless sleep.

Something wrong.

Nothing made sense anymore. She found herself talking out loud. Some half-finished thought, some re-

pressed desire pushed aside by Nathaniel's needs. She wanted to get high, like she used to do in college with Stanley, before they both dropped out. Since she'd had Elaina, even getting high seemed like it took too much energy, buying it, cleaning it, rolling it, hiding it, making sure Laney wasn't around. So she stopped.

She found herself alone.

Mama lived too far away. Stanley had been trying to run away. Since before Elaina had been born, soon as he found out he'd made Freeda pregnant. After the second one, he ran back and forth to his piece of a gas-pumping job downtown, the best he could do without a college degree, he'd remind her between sips of his favorite beer. With all the overtime he had to put in, wasn't much time left for sitting around the house making sure everyone was alright. After all, didn't she think that the parenthood thing was a little overrated? One day he just got too tired of it all to make it back home.

Then there was Elaina. A six-year-old girl trying with all her heart to be mama to her twenty-five-year-old mother.

Something wrong. Bites. Chunks taken out of her. A hole beginning somewhere.

"Too fast, Mommy. Too fast."

Freeda was running down the street now, half lift-

ing, half dragging Elaina. The water in the pot on the stove. She had put the nipples in to sterilize them.

Hours ago.

Sudden terror—deep and strong, pumping the breath out of her. She was running full tilt, Elaina in her trembling arms.

Nathaniel.

God, please don't let anything happen to my baby. Please.

Her nose was running. She touched her stomach. Looked at her hand. Felt like someone had slit her open.

A dark hole. Wider than the space that had brought Nathaniel to her.

Please. Please. Oh God.

Wide enough to fit his legs, his shoulders, his head.

The police had roped off the area.

Nathaniel. Nathaniel.

The building wrapped in flames.

"Ma'am, you're not allowed—"

"My son!"

"Ma'am." The dull mercury in the cop's eyes moving as he saw the woman look past his shoulder.

A white sheet was covering the tiny body on the ground.

"I'm sorry."

But Freeda knew she could hear Nathaniel.

She could hear him crying. She could save him. She could hear him. "Muthafucka! Let me in!" She pounded his chest. "My baby."

Let . . . me . . . in. Nathaniel. Let me . . .

Pounding . . . pounding . . .

"They said if you hadn't been smoking them marrywannas, things woulda been fine."

The front of Freeda's blouse was soaked with tears. "I tried to get in," she mumbled, staring at the wall. "I tried to save him." She put her head down on the table.

"Don't cry, Mommy." Elaina patted her on the back. "Don't cry."

"Didn't they?" Freeda's mother persisted.

"What?"

"Those reefers . . ."

"Oh, Mama. I wasn't smoking that stuff anymore then. They just brought that up so they could use it against me in court."

"Uh-huh."

Freeda's mother paused, then shook her head. "I know you don't want to hear it, Freeda, but you got to face the truth one day. Ask the Lord to forgive you. Might as well hear it from me. I don't know when your father's gonna bring himself to speak to you."

A chill came into Freeda's eyes. She felt Elaina's body

tighten on her lap. "I'm not gonna make it. I'd never let them know they were getting to me, but I can't fight it anymore. Tell you what, Mama"—she sniffed a falling tear—"if this is all you can tell me every time you come in here, why don't you stay home with Daddy? I'll get somebody else to bring Elaina to me."

Freeda had never talked to her mother like this before. Always needing her for something. Asking her for this or that. "Well, now don't go gettin' like that. I can bring Elaina by like I been doin'."

"I love you, Mama. I want to see you. But it's too much."

"Fine. Fine. If that's the way you want it."

Freeda looked at her mother across the table. Her mother was staring at an inmate near the back of the room who was hugging a gray-haired woman. Then, "Freeda Johnson," the guard up front said with a nod, knowing Freeda understood her time was up.

"Well," her mother said, smiling at Elaina, "guess we better be going. Say good-bye to Mommy."

"Do we have to?" Elaina said, frowning.

"You can come back and see me another day, sugar plum," Freeda said, drying her cheeks with her hands and opening her arms. "Be a good girl. Give me a kiss."

Elaina started crying.

"C'mon now, give me a kiss."

Elaina gave her mother a great, big, sloppy kiss on the lips. Then she gave her a tissue from her dress pocket to wipe her eyes.

"Here, Mommy!"

"Thank you, baby." She gestured to her mother. "Mama?"

Mrs. Johnson stood up, but made no movement toward her daughter.

"I love you," Freeda told her. "Try to understand."

Elaina walked out of the visiting room with Grammy. She waved to Mommy through the glass.

Freeda got up and stood on line by the door with the other women who were waiting to be strip searched. It was the price of the ticket for contact with the free world.

Can't let them see me weak. Fight. Fight. She reached deep for every particle of steel she had left. Freeda opened the tissue that her sugar plum had given her. She needed to smell her baby's scent. She was surprised when the soft yellow teardrops fell, one by one, out of the tissue and onto the floor.

The big gate opened. Elaina and Grammy walked through it to the world outside. Grammy dabbed the corner of her eye with her handkerchief. Elaina looked up at the man in the tower. He was smiling down at her. She stuck her tongue out and skipped ahead of Grammy to the car.

Bucket

Morning was still cozy 'neath evening's velvet blanket. Matthew Sr. eased out of his sleeping wife's arms. Then quietly, he slid into his jeans, undershirt, and socks. Years of working the land made him an expert at getting dressed and undressed in the dark. He accepted the familiar blindness, conscious of the angles and lines of his body, from his strong coffee thighs, all the way down to the sturdy ankles that had kept him on his feet all day during his fifty-five years. He could feel the muscles in his shoulder blades warming up as he pulled his sweatshirt over his unshaven face and down his back. Today was special. His boy was going to New York. Got him a big contract to play basketball in the pro leagues.

He sat on the edge of the bed, thinking. Tending the land was honest, backbreaking work. Satisfying to care for something, watch it grow, and know you had a hand in it. But always, there was more bill at the end of the month to pay than money to pay it. His father's father had worked the same land, each year losing another piece of it, then another, placing like cotton a little more debt in the burlap sack of his future, 'til heavy, brimming white with perfect forms of impossibility, he had transferred it to his son's young back. And so, like his father before him, Matthew Sr. had grown up beneath the load of the same sack his grandfather passed to his father. Now it belonged to him. But his son, Matt Jr., had somehow escaped.

The darkness was lifting, bit by bit. In the dim light, he looked at himself in the bureau mirror, seeing his grandfather, his father, and Matt looking back at him all at the same time. He couldn't stop himself from smiling. Today was special alright. Had to see about borrowing Cousin Pete's sports car. The rusty pickup wouldn't do. His son deserved to leave this town in style.

Morning came when the Virginia sky bathed itself in lemon juice and cotton candy. Matt Jr. stretched his long legs uncomfortably beneath the solid oak kitchen table. He poked at half of a grapefruit in front of him. He hated grapefruit. Always had. Mama insisted. Burns up the fat. Keeps you lean and strong like that Gregory man. Course he got a little carried away with his skinny self. Just eat it, boy.

No sense arguin' with her once she got on a roll. You had about as much chance as a fly beneath a swatter. Matt would be on his own soon enough. No one to tell him what to do. He put up with her babying him this one last time. Deep down, he knew he was going to be missing half his heart as soon as he walked out the door. Instead, he picked at his grapefruit, and pretended not to notice the tear Mama was quickly wiping away with the corner of her apron, as he shifted his feet and fantasized about New York.

It was all still so unreal. He had dreamed a dream and made it happen. Matthew Rawls, Jr., best college point guard in the country, first-round draft pick of the NBA.

Five weeks into training camp, Hoffman, the owner, and Coach Wilson sat in the cheap seats, high above the gym floor, watching the players practice. From that level, the giant muscles and perfect bodies weren't so intimidating— mere black spots that moved quickly in the air and on the ground. Spots that could be trapped, funneled, molded into one hard missile, fired at will or simply crushed into a powder and swept into the garbage.

Hoffman had fantasized about signing Matthew Rawls, Jr. for four years. He'd personally followed his high school and college career, even spoken to the boy's parents. Couldn't trust Dan to handle this one by himself. Irene, Hoffman's wife, had done her part by clipping every newspaper and magazine article she'd seen about Rawls.

The kid was a machine. Consistent, effortless, understood the fundamentals of the game, no attitude problems. In a word, he was "coachable." Hoffman knew if his franchise could sign him, Rawls could be groomed, seasoned, and led thundering into his prime.

Signing him had been a major coup, the nectar other coaches had fought to taste. And now, it was he, Jack Hoffman, who had the formula to take his team to glory.

"Are we gonna be ready?" Hoffman asked, cleaning his nails.

"Sure, Jack. We'll be ready." Wilson pulled on the brim of his cap. "A few problems," he admitted.

"Fix 'em." Hoffman looked up. "I don't want to hear your crap this year about complications and time. I'm building an empire. I pay you enough, Dan?"

"Well, yes."

"Damn right. We got problems. You fix 'em. Now how's that Rawls kid workin' out?"

"Fine. Fine. He's a good boy."

Matt was on the court, driving to the basket.

"Call him over. I want to talk to him."

The coach blew his whistle, then went down a few steps. "That's all for today, gentlemen. Lookin' pretty good. Matt, can you come up here for a second?"

Hoffman tingled as he watched Matt climbing the steps higher, becoming taller, then walking toward him, basketball tucked under his arm. He was a Black Adonis, this kid. Six foot six, muscle tone, and quick as a cat. The five million it took to sign him was worth the billions he'd bring in at the box office.

Hoffman patted the chair next to him. "Sit. Relax," he told Matt.

Matt let the ball slide into his hand, then gently placed it in the empty seat to his right. He sat down.

"How's it goin', son?" Hoffman smiled. "Everyone treating you alright?"

Matt's long arm reached over, his fingertips gripped the ball. The palm of his hand found comfort against the leather skin. He studied Hoffman's eyes. Tall or small, it was always in the eyes. "Yes, sir."

"Call me 'Jack,' son. Feel old when you call me 'sir.' "

"Okay, sir—Jack."

Hoffman nudged him good-naturedly. "Bet you're havin' a blast. First time, what do you fellas call it? 'Livin' large in New York'?" He lowered his voice. "And the women."

Matt rubbed the back of his neck and smiled self-consciously.

"Pretty one you got. What's her name, 'Tanya'?"

"Yeah, Tanya." His face lit up imagining hers.

"Where'd you meet her?"

"A club."

"The one near the theater district. The one you went to after the first Friday night practice. Hear it's pretty hot."

Matt's eyes widened as he looked at Hoffman.

"How did you . . . ?"

Hoffman smiled and put his arm around Matt's shoulder like a father. "She brags about you day and night to all her girlfriends."

"I don't believe this." Matt rubbed his forehead. "You spying on me? Got a camera in my bedroom too?"

"Don't be ridiculous. I have a contractual responsibility, son. It's my job to make sure you're okay—no bad food, drugs, influences. Anything that jeopardizes your future with this ballclub." He paused. "Look. Dan and I have been talking." Matt looked angrily at his coach, who looked away. "And frankly, Matt, we have some concerns about Tanya."

"What? Is she alright?"

Hoffman pulled at his lips, a habit he'd developed when he was deciding the best way to go. "No, son. She's not."

He let go of the ball.

"There's a street element she associates with. Ex-cons. Possible drug users."

Matt started to rise. "I don't believe you."

"Easy." Hoffman put his hand lightly on Matt's chest. "When I was your age, I ran a little wild too. Lotsa lady friends." His face was nearly touching Matt's, eyes sharp as pencil points. "She could jam you."

All this time everyone had made him feel like he was calling all the shots. "You the man!" they said. Matt felt as if he were a firefly suddenly crashing against the walls of a glass jar he never knew was there.

"I've been in this league a long time. I've seen it happen before, Matt."

"What are you talking about?"

"Wrong place. Wrong time. One lucky photographer looking to make a name for himself. Media would eat you up."

"You don't know her. Tanya's a good woman."

"Happens to the best of 'em."

"What are you trying to say? She's a drug addict or something?"

"I don't know what she is."

"Yeah, well, whatever she is, she ain't none of your business."

"Everything you do is my business. Tell me something: Have I ever lied to you?"

"No."

"Broken a promise?"

"No."

Matt was silent, an empty feeling rising from his stomach.

Hoffman stood up and extended his hand. "Hey. We're

glad you're part of the family." Matt looked at him. Hoffman patted him on the back. Wilson stood up. Hoffman leaned down and spoke softly in Matt's ear, "Son, I'm gonna make you a star."

Hoffman and Wilson walked away.

Matt sat there for a few minutes after they left. He looked down at his hands. *His* were the fingers that grabbed, pounded, reached, and released. *His* brain signaled, rearranged, chose the perfect moments. *His* eyes sliced the seam, kissed the sweet spot before the swish. *His* feet blurred, leaped. *His* body surged, in, out, disappearing, becoming ball and net.

His talent. Not Hoffman's.

He stood up and walked slowly back down the bleacher steps to the court. The ball boy was putting the equipment away when Matt's feet touched the wood. Matt's face was hot. He was breathing hard. Hoffman's words were poking holes in his chest. *It's my job . . . Anything . . .* He dribbled the ball, racing to the far end of the court. He neared the basket, pushed off, went straight up floating, then lingering above the rim, before he slammed the ball through the hole. He chased the rebound down, then glided to the top of the key, firing three pointers. Bucket. Bucket. Bucket.

The ball boy who had stopped to watch him was lifting a canvas sack filled with balls. Matt looked over at him. "I got it," he said, dripping sweat. He thought of his father and his grandfather before him. He picked it up, slung it across his young back, the way he'd seen it done in the field a thousand times, and slowly, determinedly, Matt Jr. headed for the locker room.

Deena

Within beauty both shores meet and all
contradictions exist side by side . . . God and
the Devil are fighting there . . .
—FEODOR DOSTOEVSKI, *THE BROTHERS KARAMAZOV*

Deena opened her eyes, slowly.

Remember dear, sleep is beauty's best friend.

The room had one window, shade down. Near the door, a pile of dirty clothes. Stacks of catalogs, restaurant delivery menus, and junk mail leaned against the beige walls. There was a bed and a dresser. The bed consisted of a box spring and a mattress. The dresser was simple, rectangular, white.

A grayness lived in almost every room of the apartment.

This morning, it permeated the bedroom and slipped beneath the rainbow comforter that Deena clutched protectively, like a shield, to her chin. The bland dullness seeped inside her, filling her with a sharp, fierce emptiness.

A frowning girl is not a pretty girl.

She slid her slender legs from beneath her covers.

Twenty-two degrees, the man on the radio said.

The clanging of the pipes was loud, as the heat struggled to break through. Deena gingerly pushed her feet into her slippers. She made her way to the bathroom.

Every day is an opportunity to become more beautiful.

A stream of sunlight pouring from beneath the bathroom door soaked her toes as she stood in front of it. She opened the door and stepped inside. She was surrounded by the thickness of the light. It seemed as if she could dip a ladle into it and drink the sun's drippings until she was full. The grayness could not live here. She removed her nightgown and immersed herself.

God had delicately hand-blown her body like a fine, crystal piece of art. He had kissed each feature upon her, and proudly pressed into creation each indentation.

Deena pulled the metal string down in front of the mirror, releasing a fluorescence that escaped into the corners of the room. She stared at her image with the usual displeasure. Her dark eyebrows needed plucking. Her eyelashes were too short. Her pink lips not full enough. Her cheeks too pale. And there were bags under her eyes.

There was something about her hair. It simply *was*. It didn't do anything. Maybe a new look. Yes, she needed to wear her hair up today. He would like that. She would *make* herself beautiful. That was the magic of this room.

Beauty is as beauty does.

The water she splashed on her face slapped her awake. Carefully, purposefully, Deena soaped. Deena scrubbed. Deena rinsed and dried. Deena brushed, then gargled. Deena lotioned, sprayed, and perfumed.

She had learned that this thing called beauty had to be worked at.

All her life, everyone had told her how beautiful she was. Her first conscious memory—she was three, bouncing along, holding Mommy's hand in the bread aisle of the supermarket:

"What a lovely child!"

"Thank you," her mother would say quietly, used to the praise, claiming it for herself.

Then there were all the cheek-pinching relatives: the weak-smiling women, the strong-eyed men. Then the teachers. She noticed they all treated her differently from the others. She was so "cute."

By high school, it was unanimous. Homecoming Queen. Dancing beneath the spotlight, applause embracing her, eyes envying her, arms of the handsomest boy in the senior class around her waist.

"She's so beautiful."

"Gorgeous."

"Perfect."

She wondered what they would say now.

This thing that everyone saw in her was some kind of force, a power she had been given but had never asked for. To Deena it seemed to exist outside of her, demanding to be daily strutted past strangers' eyes for approval.

She had never understood what she was supposed to do with it. She longed to give it away, this greedy pet that everyone loved, but only she was doomed to care for. Once she finished showing it off, and she was face to face with some unfamiliar man whose enraptured gaze left her nervous and uncomfortable, what then? It was a curse, causing people to notice her, forcing her to acknowledge those whom she had never given permission to enter her life.

Deena was completely dressed. She began putting her mascara on. The phone rang. It was him. She knew that, but to answer it now would spoil everything. She let it ring.

She looked at her reflection. Her imagination entered the mirror, pushing past the glass, plunging, deeper, deeper, piercing each transparent layer, reaching beyond. She arrived at a fantasy of what he looked like, his hair, his eyes, his nose, his lips. His raspy words became his tongue, licking the insides of her ears, making the liquid come in ticklish streams from inside her.

Their secret. She floated in the dream, satisfied and content.

The phone stopped ringing.

Gradually, one layer at a time, gliding, upward, through the silvery membranes of her thoughts, she returned.

She knew he would call again.

Deena chose just the right shade of lipstick to cover the places where she'd bitten her lips raw yesterday. Then she finished her eyes. There.

She needed to go outside.

She couldn't remember how long it had been since she'd been outside. Deena turned the light off and went to the closet. She had difficulty putting her coat on.

She began to sweat.

Fear gripped her feet and pressed down on her throat. She couldn't breathe. The power inside her urged her forward. The fear made her weaker, the nearer she came to the door.

God, help me.

Deena grabbed the handle of the lock. Gently, she leaned her forehead against the cold smoothness of the door, peering through the peephole, breathing heavily, trying desperately to still the wild pulsing in her neck.

She unlocked the door.

What if no one notices me?

She suddenly remembered the last time she had been in the street. The blue Porsche. The deep breath she had taken, before jumping in front of the car. The woman with the Christian Dior scarf who had helped her to stand up. Helped her quickly gather all her ugliness before it could be seen and put herself back together again. She wasn't sure, this time, if she could do it alone. Deena never knew what might happen to her on the street. Anyone's eyes, lips, or hands could undo her, pull the thread to send her spinning, unraveling finally, into nothingness.

She locked the door and took off her coat.

Deena looked through her mail. It was always in two piles—one for her, one for Mother. She took the letters. Mother paid the bills. It still amazed her how much their relationship had improved since she no longer went outside. She remembered the arguments they used to have when men would pay more attention to her than to her mother. Now Mother always had a kind word for her, content as she was to stop by every now and then with money and a smile, knowing her baby was "safe from the world."

Deena spent the rest of the day experimenting with different hairstyles, while she waited for the phone to ring. To calm herself, she bit off her hangnails, dipped her fingers in hydrogen peroxide and gave herself a manicure. She leafed through fashion magazines, telling herself that she was just as beautiful as the faces that stared back at her.

But it happened while she was watching TV. Breeze-like, an eerie feeling crawled across her chest. So many other women, so beautiful, more beautiful than she. He would change that. This frenzied beating of the frightened thing caught deep inside her chest. His words were hands that soothed her.

She looked at her watch. At last. The time had come. She hoped her makeup was just right.

She didn't know how it happened, but she had given him her power. And now, he fed it back to her. He enjoyed it. Each day. Let her taste it, slowly. She sipped. He shivered. More. She melted it in her mouth. More. Completely. More. He gave it to her, all the words she needed. The power had always been the words. They sizzled as she swallowed.

The things he wanted her to do to him. All the things he wanted to do to her. It was then, in those moments, that she knew how beautiful she was.

The phone rang. Deena smiled.

French

Boys liked the girl, and men were pulled in by the woman they thought they saw. Marcelle was lemongrass and long black hair. She was only sixteen.

Everyone said she was pretty. Almost as beautiful as her mother. But everybody knew that Marcelle Johnson was not giving it up. She had other things on her mind. She was French. Well, at least she had it in her. French in her blood. Something special. That's what her mama had told her.

When she was little, Granddaddy used to say, "Don't you let no sweet-talkin' little boy tell you what to do. No sir. You real special. Listen to your voices. Ones inside your head. Them ones outside you bound to get you in a heap a trouble." Marcelle didn't understand half the stuff Granddaddy said, but she loved being with him. She liked the way his voice smoothed the air around them, like the whole world was some giant cat he could fit in his hands and get to purrin' just right.

"I hear your granmama all the time. Sometimes I even see her," he would say, like he wasn't even talking to this little girl on his knee, like he was talking beyond her to the South Carolina sun setting behind the hill in his backyard. Marcelle thought it was their secret conversation while

Mommy and Daddy came in and out the backdoor, fussin' about one thing or the other.

One time, when Marcelle was listening to Granddaddy, she heard her parents arguing inside the house. But Granddaddy's stories were much more interesting than trying to figure out what they were saying.

"Dammit, Jewel. We've been through this before. I know that being here in Mama's house brings you back to the funeral. But why do you always have to bring up this same petty issue? It's over, baby. Let it go."

"Petty? How my mama looked when they put her to rest is petty?"

"Alright. I'm sorry. I didn't mean it like that."

Gary was feeling guilty now. He knew how sensitive his wife was about certain things.

"Some illiterate nigger who can't follow instructions paints Mama up like a damn ghetto whore, and that's petty?" Jewel asked, her anger toward both men—the funeral director and her husband—building into a flame that threatened to torch the house to the ground.

"Jewel . . . baby," Gary attempted.

"Don't 'Jewel, baby' me. You're just like the rest of them. Don't understand the real meaning of things. Having Mama in all that darkness—those tones against her pretty skin."

"What's that supposed to mean?"

"MY MAMA WAS NO GODDAMN NIGGER!"

Granddaddy got real quiet. The gray steps of the porch were a few feet behind them, swallowed up by shadows alive with fireflies and crickets. Marcelle and Granddaddy were drinking iced tea. Marcelle stirred hers with a spoon, trying to make the sugar crystals that had settled beneath the ice cubes melt into the tobacco-colored liquid.

Finally, Granddaddy spoke. "You your granmama. She passed her looks on to you."

"I look like Granmama? Really?" This pleased her. No one ever had anything to say about Granmama that wasn't a compliment.

"Sure as I'm sittin' here, talkin' to you, your granmama is lookin' straight at me. Through your eyes. She was special alright." Granddaddy let half a smile crawl up his tan cheek.

"Everybody wanted to be her fella," he continued. "But couldn't nobody get close to her. She wouldn't let 'em. I watched the way she'd walked down through the center of this town and take half the population with her. The men and boys, that is. Women never had the patience for her. They was jealous.

"At first your granmama paid me 'bout as much attention as a sidewalk do a snowflake in winter. Then I bought a dozen roses. Sent her one each day, with a little card. By the time she got Rose Number Twelve, she was in love with me without even knowing who I was. After our first date, we made plans to get engaged, and by our fourth date, we was married."

Sometimes Granddaddy would explain how Granmama was like a wise and beautiful Indian spirit, a goddess who had warriors killing each other to be her one-and-only. Indian braves honored to fertilize the floor of the forest in quest of her love.

Yeah. Marcelle was a French Indian.

That's what she was trying to tell Ida, her best friend, as they sat at the big, round table in the high school library. They were supposed to be researching about how something called "chlorophyll" was involved with something else called "photosynthesis." Ida told Marcelle it would all be clearer once they copied it down, word for word, from the fat brown encyclopedia.

"But, Ida, I don't understand what all these words mean. Besides, what do you think about what I told you?"

Ida scrunched up her face.

"About me being a French Indian!"

"Young lady," began Miss Coppinger, the librarian, "there are other, serious people here who would like to study." Then she lowered her glasses and squinted over the top of them at Ida. Ida stared back without a blink.

"And what is *your* name?" she asked Ida.

"What's it to ya?" Ida mumbled under her breath.

Marcelle giggled and couldn't stop until Ida pinched her under the table.

"I can't hear you, young lady," Miss Coppinger said.

Ida started to suggest a hearing aid, but changed her mind.

"My name is Ida Harris," she said as loudly as she could. Then she stood up. "And my father is President of the Wilson Heights N-double-A-C-P."

"Well . . . well, just keep your voice down, please."

"Long as you say 'please,' " Ida said, then smiled.

She sat back down and winked at Marcelle, who had her hand over her mouth to keep her laugh from bursting out.

That was why they were such good friends. Ida had the nerve to say and do everything Marcelle didn't. Looking at the two of them—Ida, big-boned and dark-skinned, and Marcelle, fragile and high yaller—you'd never imagine that they were sisters in each other's eyes.

"Why can't you bring home some of your other friends?" Marcelle's mother had asked.

"But, Mama, Ida is my best, best friend," Marcelle had answered.

"I know, honey. I would just like to meet some of your other, well, you know, your different friends."

Ida ripped a piece of paper from her notebook. She lowered her head and started scribbling like a crazy woman. Marcelle pulled her chair closer and leaned on her friend's shoulder. Ida had the kind of hair that turns into tiny, kinky balls at the back of the neck, and as she scribbled, some of the sweat dropped down and fell into the balls, making them glisten like black pearls against velvet. Marcelle loved to watch Ida draw. She was fascinated by the way her pencil could give birth to one weird-looking line, then another, adding and changing them, sending them wiggling back and forth across the paper. Ida was drawing her favorite cartoon character, "Keep-Quiet Coppinger." Marcelle silently accepted the fact that Ida was going to get them in trouble—again.

Like the time she was supposed to meet her during sixth period, in the bathroom by the gym . . .

Where the hell was Ida? Marcelle would kill her when she found her.

She wasn't in the gym. Maybe she'd be in the lounge. Marcelle looked up and down the halls, into classrooms. She reached the lounge just in time to see the back of Ida's head pressed up against the glass in the wooden door.

Marcelle wasn't sure what was going on. There were

all sorts of strange, whispered sounds. She saw Junior, the cutest guy at Frederick Douglass, close to Ida, his arms around her. She was suddenly dizzy. Her body felt hot. Junior was kissing Ida so hard, his eyes were closed in total concentration.

Marcelle was fascinated, yet repulsed. She felt like something else was going on in there that she couldn't see, that she didn't understand. Her mother had told her that only dirty girls who wanted to get pregnant got all hugged up with boys, like Ida was doing, right here before her eyes.

Marcelle didn't know what to think. What to feel. All she knew was that she didn't want them to see her, didn't want anyone to see her standing there watching them do whatever they were doing. She ran.

The library was suddenly quiet. Everyone was listening for the same thing. The bell rang.

"Shucks," Ida said, in the middle of drawing a bird about to make a deposit on Coppinger's head. "I was almost done."

When they were standing in the hallway, Marcelle turned, facing Ida.

"Well?" she asked.

"Well what?"

"You know what."

Ida looked at her like she had lost her mind. "Marcy, I don't know what you're talking about."

"Me. Me being a French Indian."

"Oh, girl. You ain't no damn French woman. You half as dark as me and can't speak a word a French."

"That don't mean nothing. You just jealous."

They moved with the crowd, which as usual, was squeezing itself through the two front doors of the school.

"Jealous?" Ida answered loudly. She had a talent for one-word performances, her face and body a sideshow of rhythms and expressions.

A few people standing on the steps outside looked in their direction.

"Jealous?" Ida repeated. " 'Bout bein' some Euro-peon? Not this Ida here. Must be talkin' 'bout some other Ida. Indian I could believe. Ain't met no Black folk yet ain't got some Indian in 'em somewhere. But how that make you French?"

"I ain't hardly got to explain this to *you*, Ida Harris."

"Well excuse me for tryin' to figure out your simple black ass in the first place."

"You don't have to get stink about it."

"Look who's talkin' 'bout stink—Miss Stink White Girl French Indian USA."

Somebody laughed. Marcelle wanted to hit Ida. She

wanted to slap her for making fun of all those magic nights, sometimes on Mama's lap, other times on Granddaddy's knee, when each word of every story had tickled and kissed her ears and made her feel so special.

There was a crowd now, and it wanted to be fed.

The feelings inside Marcelle bubbled hot, threatening to spill into the cracks of the sidewalk.

"FIGHT! FIGHT!" someone said, signaling the others.

"What'chyou gon' do? You gon' hit me, Miss Stinky Pants?" Ida taunted.

Marcelle knew that she could never beat Ida in a fistfight. She had been taught that only a lower-class person would fight anyway. So she walked away, leaving Ida standing in front of the school with her hands on her fighting hips and nobody to fight. She felt the darts of Ida's words dig into her back, but she kept walking. She made it past the tall iron gates of the school entrance, and into the street.

Marcelle wondered why she was friends with Ida anyhow. She acted so thickheaded sometimes. Like that bad, nappy hair of hers took over her brain.

"How's ma girl today?" Mr. Howard asked, passing by and smelling of blackberry brandy. He still had his cap on from work, and drops of paint were splattered against his coconut shell–colored hands and face, and all over his uniform. Granddaddy say, man work that hard day in, day out, grow to be proud of not caring how he looked. Go anywhere in his workclothes.

"Fine, Mr. Howard," Marcelle answered, still thinking about Ida.

"How's your mama doin', alright?"

"Fine."

"You tell her Mr. Howard said"—he looked away, then back at Marcelle—"you tell her I said, 'Hello,' y'hear?"

"Yessir."

"Don't you forget now."

"I won't."

To get home, Marcelle had to walk down Main Street. Usually, when she was with Ida, she could pretend she was a royal lady of the French court, strolling among the bowing, countryside peasants, who welcomed this moment, however brief, to brush against the hem of her aristocratic gown.

Today she felt something quiver inside her, as she passed the abandoned building next to the liquor store with all the men crowded on the sidewalk in front of it like roaches to garbage. Today Marcelle could not avoid their eyes. No magic shields today, no silk queen masks to hide her from them or them from her. Her lips froze, and the quivering tightened until it became a suctioning cavity above her breasts, pulling closer, all the smells, all the sounds, and all the sights that she had never let in.

The men smelled of cheap wine, urine, and sadness. Eyes briefly brightened by the liquid fire racing death inside them. Red faces. Green bottles. Hands swollen. Lips cracked.

"Hey shurgah."

"Lord have mercy. Look-a-here."

Whistles. Eyes like hands on her breasts and on her behind. And now a man reached out to touch her.

"Ah walk wid ya, swee'har'."

Marcelle stepped quickly to the corner, past the store, past the barber shop across the street, which had an equal share of tar and caramel men who followed the movement of her body with their own. The voice was beginning to blend back into the tapestry from which it came.

"Ah on'y wan' walk wid ya, bitch."

Snakes. Marcelle tried not to think of the snakes. She had dreamt of them two nights before. She had wanted to scream, to vomit, but she ran on and on in the dark, past the trees and rocks. Snakes were falling, crawling up her dress, down her throat and back. She cried out for help. Somebody. But the slick sound of thousands of snakes moving against the leaves and each other got louder and louder . . .

"LORD! SWEET JESUS. PRAISE. PRAISE. PRAISE HIS NAME."

The music of an organ flung the street sounds aside as Marcelle walked past The Holy Church of God. Through the open doors, colors jerked back and forth, brown hands clapped, shoes shiny black stomped, shouts jumped, slid down walls, rolled from one side of the church to the other.

"PRAISE GOD!"

There was a funeral parlor to pass before the cleaners and then home. Something made her look to her right. Something was there.

It was a charcoal-colored figure, the head wrapped in cloth of purple and blue, looking out from the window of what used to be a candy store. It called her. Soundlessly. With the index finger of the right hand. Something for her eyes only. Something necessary.

Marcelle hesitated, but was overtaken by her curiosity. As she came closer to the window, the figure disappeared. Marcelle strained to look through the glass, but could only see the darkness. She turned to move away.

"I have something to show you," the darkness said.

Something bristled the hairs on her arms. A grayish light became a candle. Marcelle thought she could see a woman's shape sitting next to a tall cardboard box. There was a small wooden chair. She wanted to run. Instead, she entered.

"Sit, Marcelle," the woman said. "Rest."

"How do you . . ." Marcelle asked, as the quivering regained control of her body, ". . . know my name?"

"There are many things I know more important than your name."

Life had made the woman old, her girlish spirit snatched and swallowed. But somewhere, in between her wrinkles, Marcelle found something familiar. The face reminded her of Granmama. But that couldn't be. Granmama had never been this color.

"I have watched you," the woman said. "Your friend?"

Marcelle was cautious, not knowing why she felt she should answer this woman.

"She had something else to do today."

"She is very pretty."

Marcelle scraped her feet back and forth across the floor. Never had she thought of Ida in that way. Ida was just Ida, funny but dark.

"Why have you been watching us?" she asked.

"I watch everything," the woman answered.

The room was small, entombed in the quiet, the blackness, and the smell of burning incense. There was a dirt-stained, orange sleeping bag in one corner and a supermarket shopping cart in the other. The floor had holes in some places, and every now and then, something scurried by.

Marcelle felt cold fear touch at her stomach and throat.

She heard it growl in her ears. Her parents' house seemed distant, unreachable, and for a moment, she wondered if she would ever see it again. She needed to hear a sound, any sound that she recognized. Perhaps, if she could sacrifice her voice to the silence.

"Why . . . ?" she asked, but her offering sounded like the voice of someone else, "What do you want?"

The woman looked up quickly at Marcelle, as if she had been interrupted from a conversation with another. She pointed across the room. "Look in that mirror, girl. Tell me what you see."

Marcelle stood up and slowly walked toward a chipped mirror. It reflected the faint light from the candle. Her features appeared uneven; her skin, dark.

"I don't know. I mean . . . I see me, Marcelle."

"Who are you, child?"

"I'm me."

"WHO ARE YOU?"

"I don't know what you mean. I don't understand." She was crying. "Who are *you*?"

The woman stood next to her and looked with her into the mirror. "Do you look like me?" she asked.

"No. I'm . . ."

"You're what?"

"I'm lighter. I'm . . ."

"When I was your age, I was ten times prettier."

Marcelle was shocked. She looked away from the mirror. She didn't know what to say.

The woman continued. "I could have had any boy I wanted, Black or white. But—" She paused. "I didn't."

"Why not?"

"I was only the one they desired in their dreams. No one dared be seen with me. 'She's too Black,' they'd say."

"Why are you telling me this?"

"Because no one talked to me about it. Are your parents white, child?"

"No."

"I thought not. You have the look of an African woman."

"No. My granmama was a French Indian. Grandaddy told me."

"A fantasy to keep you chasing someone else's ghosts."

"My grandaddy don't lie."

"He told you what he believed."

"It's true!"

The woman held Marcelle's face lovingly between her palms, and gently turned Marcelle back to the mirror.

"Look at us, girl. You and I, we are the same. African."

As Marcelle watched, the old woman's features transformed, betrayed her past, and for a moment, showed the beauty, awesome and unique, that had once possessed her.

Astonished, Marcelle could not help herself. She wanted to touch the woman's face. "You *are* beautiful," she said.

"As you will one day be. But you will be beautiful not because you are light. You will be beautiful because you are Black. We come in many colors. All beautiful." She stood behind her, so that her image in the mirror rested above Marcelle's. "When you see yourself," she said, "think of me." But then, she began to move closer, as if to embrace her.

Marcelle tensed, feeling trapped. The spell was broken.

The woman's sweaty, unwashed smell began to choke Marcelle. "We have missed you, princess," the woman said, holding her arms open.

Marcelle pushed the old woman away from her. She was terrified. She had to get out. The woman almost fell, but was stronger than Marcelle expected, and reached out and grabbed Marcelle's arm.

"Let go of me!" Marcelle screamed.

The woman put her hand over Marcelle's mouth. "I'm not going to hurt you, but you must not scream. The police will come and I have no place else to go. Will you be quiet now?"

Marcelle nodded.

"I took a chance with you," the woman said, still holding her arm. "Perhaps it was too soon. I mean you no harm. One day, when you are old like me, you may understand. I did

146

what I did because you belong. I love you." She let go of her, walked to the box where the candle was, blew it out, then seemed to disappear.

Marcelle frantically felt along the wall with her hands. It was rawly constructed, and scratched the tips of her fingers. She heard the scampering of something large near her feet. Eventually, she found the doorway.

She was crying when she made it outside to the front of the building. The same, old voice told Marcelle to run. A new voice gently held her hand. "Breathe," it said. "You'll be just fine." Marcelle wiped her eyes with the back of her hand and stepped back from the building to see where she had been. It looked exactly as it had when she first noticed it, empty.

Marcelle began walking. Her feet knew the way, and took her in the direction of her home. She passed the cleaners, and made it to her block. She didn't hear Mr. Bullard when he yelled "Evening, princess" from the doorway of the grocery store across the street from her house.

The lights were on in the dining room where her mother had eaten dinner with a neighbor, Miss Williams. Dinner finished, the two were seated, sipping brandy, smoking, and talking.

"Marcelle"—her mother stood up as Marcelle walked in the room—"where have you been? I must have called your father fifty times tonight asking him if he knew what happened to you."

"I came from school," Marcelle responded, picturing herself asleep upstairs.

"It took you all this time to get from school home? Something's missing here, young lady."

She started to tell her the truth, but decided that this truth belonged to her. She chose to keep it in her secret inside place where she could replay it, re-feel it, understand what had happened. Well, only Ida could know. She couldn't wait to tell her. "Honest, mama"—she began moving toward the stairs—"all I did was walk home. Can I use the upstairs phone?"

Her mother stood perfectly still and studied Marcelle's face. "Marcelle. You sure there's nothing else you want to tell me?"

"Yes, Mama." Marcelle sighed.

"Alright. You must be starving. I'll just warm up this meat—"

"I'm not hungry."

"Not hungry? Are you feeling alright, baby?"

"Yes. May I go upstairs?"

"Sure, honey. I'll be up later."

"Goodnight, Mama. Goodnight, Miss Williams."

Marcelle walked a few feet, then stopped.

"Oh. Mama."

"Yes?"

"I almost forgot to tell you. Mr. Howard said 'Hello.' "

Jewel Johnson's eyes were suddenly black-handled scissors, shining and cutting the air around her. She stroked her silky hair and said, "That black nigger? Hmph!"

Alice & Jesse

The aroma of honeyed ham, gravied turkey, fried chicken, potato salad, and magic hot rolls that made butter slide off the knife and disappear, filled Miss Douglass's house. The funeral was over. The adults would eventually get pleasantly smashed from a mixture of memories and booze, the older women sitting at the kitchen table, resting patient, weary feet, unaware of the silver strands that had found a way to peek out from beneath their loosened wigs, the younger ones huddled excitedly in corners, laughing self-consciously, whispering the closed-bedroom-door secrets of new womanhood, and the men, with tie-discarded shirts open at the collar, sharing smoke and Scotch-brewed conversations, forgetting, for a moment, the children, their sons and daughters, who had taken the opportunity to vanish and enjoy their unattended freedom.

Alice was in the bathroom. She was carefully spraying herself with her first bottle of perfume she'd saved her money to buy at the five-and-ten-cent store. She touched her cream soda–colored fingertips to the wet excess on her neck, then dabbed herself lightly behind her ears, the way she'd seen glamorous women do in the movies. She looked directly into the mirror. Maybe she *was* as pretty as Daddy said she was. Alice leaned away from, then into the mirror to achieve the proper angle for kissing. Closer, closer to the lips of the man of her dreams. The eye-closing moment was near, the moment when he kissed her. Blindly, lost in ecstasy, she left her steamy, lip-shaped mark.

Jesse opened his eyes. He was in the basement, sitting on the couch. His head was slightly bowed toward the floor, his legs apart. This house belonged to his mother now that Grandma was gone. He never knew his grandfather. From the time he was little, he could remember Grandma hugging him and saying he was the man in her life. Everyone knew how much he had loved her.

Upstairs, Uncle Ellis had grabbed his shoulder tightly with one hand and shoved a drink under his nose with the other, like a doctor prescribing medicine. Jesse had politely refused. How could he explain to his uncles and his father that he needed to talk? Not about football, women, and politics, but about what he was feeling? Or maybe he didn't need to talk, just let himself feel, release the silent conversation one tear at a time.

But these men never talked. They boasted, joked, and drank away their pain. Sharing, crying—those things were for women. Men stopped being men when they opened the doors to all those private rooms they never talked about, but knew were a part of the house. Grandma not only knew about the rooms, she'd tell you what was in them and help you re-decorate. They said she was crazy. Jesse knew better. Grandma was the keeper of the secrets.

He listened for her now. Maybe she could tell him why he felt compelled to come to the basement, away from the others, why his instincts were telling him that whatever needed to happen to make him feel better would happen here, in this room.

"I'm sorry about your grandmother."

Jesse looked up, his thoughts interrupted by this stranger, this girl standing in front of him.

Earlier, she had seen him go downstairs. She had waited, finally gathering the nerve to follow him into the quiet, ignoring his apparent need to be alone.

He leaned back against the couch and closed his eyes. *Maybe she'll go away.*

She stood awkwardly in front of him, the plate of food she had fixed in her hand. She looked more closely at his face. She wasn't sure, but she thought he'd been crying. She decided to put the plate on the table next to him.

"My name is Alice. I brought you something to eat."

Slowly, he opened his eyes and stared at her, loud in his focused silence.

"Did I say something wrong?"

She backed away from his glare.

"I'm sorry if—"

"No."

"Then what?"

"I'm really not hungry. I want to be by myself. And besides, nobody ever fixes my plate in this house except my grandmother."

"Oh. I'm sorry. I didn't mean . . ."

"Moms always says, 'You grown enough to fix your own plate.' But Grandma, she fixes it for me anyway. She always . . ." He turned away from her. "Damn." He stood up, and faced the wall. The tears spilled down his cheeks, wetting his white shirt, spotting his tie. "It's none of your business," he said.

Alice knew she should feel uncomfortable, looking at him with his back to her. She didn't. She didn't care. Jesse was just too fine. Being in the same room with him was enough. Alice decided to sit in a chair a few feet away. She cupped her face in her hands and leaned in his direction, digging her elbows into her knees, studying him like he was a curious treasure she had discovered.

He looked over his shoulder. "What you lookin' at?" he asked.

"You."

"Didn't your mama teach you it's not polite to stare?"

"Yeah. So?"

"So cut it out."

"Okay . . . So. Wanna talk about it?"

"What are you, a shrink or something?"

"No, I just thought you . . ."

"I don't even know you."

". . . snotty about it. I'm just trying to—"

"And even if I did know you, I wouldn't want to talk to *you* anyway. Leave me alone."

Alice couldn't stop the hot, embarrassed tears that were forming in her eyes. She liked him and he didn't like her. He had hurt her on purpose. She stood up, defeated, and walked toward the door.

"I was only trying to be your friend," she said softly.

"Wait. I'm sorry. It's not you. My grandmother . . . I . . . I don't feel like being around anybody right now. I just don't feel like talking."

"I'll be quiet. I won't bother you. I promise, Jesse."

"Who told you my name?"

"Everybody knows who *you* are, Jesse. Besides, I know lots of things."

"What things?"

"Things. That's all."

"Like what?"

"Like how people feel. They don't have to say anything. I can feel it. Sometimes it's like something inside them is whispering to something inside me." She sat back down beside him. "Why don't you eat? You'll feel better."

Jesse looked at the plate of food between them. It looked good, but he knew it could not fill the numb and empty place inside him.

"I'm not hungry."

"*I* made the chicken." She grinned, passing him a drumstick. "One tiny bite?"

He looked at it. Reluctantly, he took it and nibbled on the end. He couldn't taste anything.

"You like it?"

"It's okay."

They sat for a long time, Jesse picking at his food, Alice watching, not knowing what to say next.

"You loved her very much, didn't you?" she ventured.

Just when it was starting to feel better, here she was making him feel the pain all over again.

"I told you. I don't want to talk about it."

"I know that you loved her. It's still here in this room."

"What?"

"The love. I can feel it. She loved you too. A lot."

"Shut up!" He threw his knife at the wall on the other side of the room, then looked directly at her. "Just shut up! You don't know anything about it. Nobody knows. It was . . ."

He blinked a tear down his cheek.

"It was . . . She was . . ."

All of it needed to pour out of him. The flow was stronger than the dam he had tried so hard to build.

"She understood me. I could talk to her about anything. She never criticized me. Even when I was wrong. Nobody else was like her. There's no one . . ." He let his tears keep coming. ". . . I . . . don't understand why she had to leave me. It was like we had this secret thing between us. She told me . . . she would always be here for me."

The palms of his hands touched his wet cheeks. He leaned forward and covered his eyes, and surrendered. The moment dragged the emptiness out of him, teaching him how to release it. Just for now, just this moment. Helping him push it. Out. Feel it. Flow. Breath by breath, away from him. His head fell back against the couch. He held on, dug his nails into the palm of his left hand. Slowly, felt his jaw unclench. Little by little, he became aware of her, massaging the numbness, reshaping the pain into soothing circles slowly, firmly, until the river was a trickling absorbed by the tissue Alice placed gently in his hand.

He wiped his eyes.

"Thanks." He gave her an awkward kiss on the forehead. His eyes looked at her face for the first time and his lips found their way softly, tenderly to hers.

As Alice felt herself pulled toward him, she was pulled back by her mother's face.

"You never kissed a boy before, have you?"

"Sure I have. Lots of times," she said, trying to sound grown-up.

He stroked her cheek with the back of his hand. "I like you, Alice. I'm not going to hurt you."

He held her hand as they stood up, facing each other. He pulled her to him, and kissed her again.

This time his kiss held her, reminding her of all the childhood, sweet tastes and smells that had kept her an enchanted, willing prisoner of Mama's kitchen—the vanilla, the pudding, the liquid, sugared ingredients invisibly baking themselves into a cake. Jesse was the chocolate frosting left for her on the sides of the bowl.

Inside Out

William ran into a bookstore on Franklin Street. That extra roll around his midsection made him work much harder than he cared to admit. He was safe. At least for a few minutes anyway. He stayed alert in the Business Section, just in case the man from whom he was running happened to appear behind a copy of the bestseller *Using Power Meetings to Effectively Mask Your Impotence.*

He wasn't terribly tall, this man whom William feared, but he was Black like William. Not a particularly menacing face, perhaps even sympathetic under a different set of circumstances. What was frightening was his relentlessness. What was haunting was his familiarity. Had William the courage to walk right up and ask him what business he had following him, William was sure he would recognize him. There was something reminiscent about the straw cap, brown cotton short-sleeve shirt with the white trim down the center, shiny white buttons, black pants, and the lewd swagger of his hips advertising the pride between his legs.

The man would always be waiting for him, leaning against a wall of an office building or resting on a bench near the T, arms stretched out behind him, legs spread apart. He never spoke. (After all, these were the nineties and they were in downtown Boston.) At first, he'd simply stare at William.

Sometimes he'd shake his head like the old folks did when a power greater than their own slapped them with a sudden truth. Eventually, he'd begin to move toward William. He never came too close, but always close enough for William to see him, at every other block, when he looked nervously over his right shoulder.

William loosened his tie and began thumbing through *Business Zen & the Art of Career Maintenance*.

> *As a dollar on the river of life, flow with the go.*
> *Fill your hands. Empty your mind.*

He put it back on the shelf. As he browsed, he found an old and dear friend—*Lose Your Accent in Ten Easy Lessons*. William reached for the book and remembered when he had first bought it four years ago.

It had been on a Friday night. Mid-July. The financial district was empty, bankers and brokers having left to get bitten by expensive Cape Cod mosquitoes.

William had been lonely. There was only one other Black man in the office where he worked. He had promptly looked William over on the day of William's arrival, and since then, had avoided him at every turn. Occasionally, William would notice one or two white employees watching him from a distance, as if he were a bad accident that had happened to their workplace.

No one ever talked to him, unless they had to. When they did, they'd stare at the width, wonder at the depth of his African American lips, watch them moving, then wait for a translation. William would try so hard to explain himself in a way they could understand. (No exact translation for chitlins and black-eye peas.) They'd politely excuse themselves and he would silently promise to try harder next time.

Poor, lonely William. He didn't want to go home to Maybelle, his wife, that night in July. He was tired of fighting with her about changing her ways. No matter where they went, she'd always manage to find some Black person. Mix that chocolate with vanilla, you still got chocolate, she'd say. What was wrong with her? Didn't she know that when they attended social events at his job, it didn't look good for him if there were too many of them in the crowd?

They were in Boston now, not Mobile. Things were different here. Didn't she want to make something of herself? Didn't she want to be *accepted*? Well then, she'd have to make an effort to make these people who had no color feel more comfortable by not acting so . . . so . . . well, colored. They'd been through it a thousand times.

The alienation, the humiliation, all of it had been vibrating through William's mind and soul that night when he happened upon *Lose Your Accent in Ten Easy Lessons*.

Black as William was, God *did* love him. This was his answer.

For three hours every night, he spoke the words out loud, he practiced, he enunciated, he repeated, he drove Maybelle crazy. In a little over a week, he had flattened his colorful Southern dialect into a proper, gray, dry, Bostonian pancake. William stopped worrying about them staring at him and began to study them instead.

One morning he woke up, and Maybelle didn't know who he was. He had it. The air. The clothes. The speech. The attitude. The hair was a bit of a problem. The only thing he couldn't change was the skin color. Yes, it seemed like William had been on his way to real success . . .

It finally seemed safe to leave the bookstore. Surely the man had gone away by now. William headed back to the office to get his briefcase. It was here on the street that he had taught himself not to see any of them, those who looked exactly like he did. No eye contact. That was the trick. After all, what right had they to pull him back into the barrel with a simple hello, after he had worked so hard to climb out?

He took the Orange Line to Forest Hills and drove away to his *West* Roxbury home. It was a quiet evening. After dinner, Maybelle retired early, complaining of back pains. William flipped through his one hundred plus channels, finding nothing to watch. It was in the bathroom, as he was brushing his teeth in the mirror, that he saw him.

He almost choked on the toothpaste. He looked away,

dropped his toothbrush. He folded his body into a shivering little ball in a corner of the bathroom. If he didn't look, the man would go away. William rocked back and forth, waiting for the man to disappear.

A few minutes later, on his hands and knees, he slowly crept along the floor toward the sink. Then, as if to capture a sleeping enemy, he peered cautiously over the bottom edge of the mirror. The man's eyes were right there, watching. William ducked quickly out of view and slid down to the floor, his back to the sink. His right cheek began to twitch. It seemed like he could feel his heartbeat in every part of his body. He placed his hand against his chest. He had to try and get himself together.

Gaining the courage to look closer, William went back to the mirror. He knew at once who the man was. He ran from the bathroom.

Maybelle was reading in bed, a heating pad between her back and her pillow.

As soon as she saw her husband, she knew what she had to do. "Now, now, honey. It's alright. Come to Mama," she said, gesturing to him. She held him close. She used the soft-ness of her finger to gently wipe the toothpaste from his lips, and the corners of his mouth. Then she rocked him in her arms. "It's gonna be alright," she told him.

He closed his eyes and dreamed of the farm back home.

The food, the warmth, the earth, the brown hands that each year had gently planted trusting seeds, free to grow inside him. He dreamed of the cold fried-chicken picnics, late night whist games, how the cool air smelled sitting on Bennie's porch at all those house parties, Mama and Daddy, his brothers and Sister Gina, his childhood friends, cousins, aunts, and uncles who loved him. Really loved him. He let all of what belonged to him back in. He dreamed. He cried. He moaned.

"It's alright, baby," Maybelle whispered, stroking his brow. "You home now. You finally home."

Joey Falling

It is happening again. Little Joey, by himself, exploring the ledge of the terrace. She cannot explain why she is not with him, why she is in the living room, watching. Little Joey. His fingers grabbing the flower box on the terrace to help him stand up. The narrow concrete overlooking the street. Don't look down, she wants to tell him. But no words come out.

One tiny foot in front of the other. Look. Way up. High. Pretty, pretty. Bird. Touch. Bird, Mommy. Jump, jump. Look.

I fly.

Joey falling. Falling. Faster. Faster. Faster and faster past each balcony of the apartment building. It is too late. He is falling. Too fast. Baby blond hair flying. His tiny fingernails grab empty bunches of wind. He screams. Something tugs at the inside of her belly—tighter, tighter. Instinctively, she tries to brace her son for the impact of the concrete. She fights not to give in to the dead space inside her chest where she knows she cannot save him.

Little Joey's three-year-old body is being pulled, down to the street. Someone should be reaching out their arms to catch him, stop him. Instead, God's finger

stretches Joey farther and farther down, like a huge rub-
ber band that will quickly send him into the shadowy
clouds of heaven.

It always happens this way. Not a step, not a word to save him. Always the same feeling surging up from her stomach, flooding her throat, leaving Marilyn bent over the toilet, try-ing to empty herself of the dream. She flushes, then studies her reflection in the mirror. Her wild dark hair frames the terror in her deep brown eyes. Intense flecks of darkness in an otherwise haggard, pale face.

She is pregnant. Again. She hasn't had the test yet, but her body remembers all the signs.

None of that matters right now.

Marilyn has overslept. She has exactly sixty minutes to eat, dress, and get to work. She hates her students to be in the room before she gets there, but this morning she'll have to live with it. Their faces always disappoint her—dull, tolerant, dispassionate, as if they were all sitting in an auto body shop waiting for their cars to be repaired, tapping their feet to beats she cannot follow, crushing their boredom like lit cig-arettes, deep into the floor. Granted, it is only Biology 101, the course none of her colleagues want to teach, but Marilyn still hopes to find, more than once in a while, a student who is alive.

She remembers when her own teachers began the cutting. Little pieces of her spirit severed and thrown away. Kindergarten with Mrs. McGarry. When to play, how to play, what not to say. More grades, more pieces. They had to make her just right. Had to fit her just so into the box. Was it so surprising that her own students were lobotomized by the time they got to college?

"Mommy! Mommy!" It's Little Joey.

Now she would really be late.

"Mommy!"

"What?"

"I have to go pee-pee."

"So get up and go pee-pee, Joey."

"Come?"

"No, Joey. I can't. I have to go to work."

Now he is wailing. "Can't do it. Help, Mommy."

"Honey, I'm late. I can't."

"Please?"

Marilyn knows that Joe is lying in bed, listening. Why the hell doesn't he get up and tend to Joey? Why is it always *her* job?

"Okay, Joey. I'm coming," she says, the veins in her neck about to burst.

Marilyn is sitting in the cafeteria, staring out of the big glass window at a tree. The air is moist with spring's seduction. Winter no longer resists the stubby blades of grass, bushes, giddy dots of green, the bulbs planted deep and warm, their promise silent, sweet.

She had met Imani in the spring. Young, gorgeous, African American woman. Nose ring, long dreads, and bright colors. Marilyn had never had a Black friend before. She thought Imani was a student at first.

"Quad this way?" Imani had asked. "Campus don't make no sense. Shoulda hired Benjamin." She reached up to break a blossom off a tree. She smelled it and closed her eyes.

"Who?"

"Benjamin Banneker? Designed D.C.?"

"Oh. I, uh, I have a map. We can look at it together," Marilyn had offered.

"Thank you, Jesus! A woman with a map!"

"Where are you going? I have a meeting in that direction."

"You too? Intellectual masturbation convention for faculty, right? We must be colleagues." She giggled, extending her hand. "Imani Brown, Chemistry. New kid on the block."

And that was how it began. Imani delighted her, a smile of motion and light in a world of gray. Like being back in junior high school, she had someone to pass notes and shoot looks to across a room of oh-so-serious scholars. She'd lower her head and smile whenever Imani entered a room, charging the air with exotic oils, bangles, and an intelligence this small town faculty was never ready for.

The dishes rattle, as the conveyor belt sends the trays into the cafeteria kitchen. Marilyn is still at the table, staring out. She sees herself inside the tree, unable to breathe against the thick bark walls. It takes a while before she realizes that Imani is standing over her. "Imani!" she finally says. "How long have you been there?"

She slides her leather backpack off her shoulders and into the chair next to Marilyn. She puts her hand on Marilyn's shoulder. "I been standing there long enough to see you ain't really here. Is it that bad?"

"Worse." Marilyn jabs her tuna with her fork. "But I won't burden you."

"Oh boy. Here we go." Imani looks through her, then past her. "Be right back. Want something?"

"All set. Thanks."

Imani returns with a tray full of food, then sits next to Marilyn. "You know, you white folks are crazy," she says, shaking her head. "You pull out a cookbook, follow the directions, make something, and throw it in the oven. Then you act like nothin's cookin'."

"What?"

"Then"—Imani dips a french fry in a pool of ketchup—"you leave the stuff in all that heat for days. It blows up. Big mess. And you sit around all dramatic trying to figure out why the whole thing happened."

"Want to give me a clue about what you're talkin' about?"

Imani holds Marilyn's eyes with her own. "I been knowing you long enough to know you don't trust easy. Someone got to give you a piece of their heart first. Let me give you a piece of mine." She touches Marilyn's hand. "I love you, girl, *I'm* your friend, remember? I know when something's wrong."

Marilyn squeezes her paper napkin into a tight ball.

"Imani. I'm pregnant." She lowers her head, strokes her forehead, then looks up. "Why are you looking at me like that?"

"That's great news. Isn't it?"

"I don't know. Now you're making me feel guilty."

"Sometimes I look at women in the street with their babies," Imani half mumbles between bites of her veggie burger. "It looks so beautiful. I feel like I just gotta have it. You know. The whole thing. Good man. Baby. Great career. Finally got up the nerve to tell that to Dennis. Haven't heard from him since.

"But you, Marilyn, I know it sounds corny, but you really do have it all." Imani looks at her watch. "Jeez. I gotta get to the airport. You remember. Biogenetics conference. Colorado. They all want to meet this little colored girl who's discovered the secret formula to make them all multibillionaires." She empties her tray, then stops. "You do know you don't have to deal with what you're feeling by yourself,

Marilyn. I don't care what time it is. You want to talk, call me at the hotel."

"Have fun," Marilyn offers half-heartedly.

"You call me. Y'hear?" Imani says on her way out the door. "I'll probably be bored to tears."

Marilyn watches her walk away. What a luxury. To actually get on a plane and go somewhere.

". . . you really, you really do have it all."

She hasn't told Joe about the baby. She knows what he will say. Bad timing. Not that he doesn't want children, not that he doesn't love children, he just doesn't want them right now. He didn't want Little Joey either, but Little Joey had come anyway.

"I thought we had an understanding, Marilyn."

"But Joe. We're married."

"What about all our plans?"

"We'll be together. Somehow, it'll work out. We'll be alright."

"Just like every other Joe Schmo in America who never got out of the starting gate. I can't believe this is happening to me."

"To us, Joe. It's happening to us. I didn't do this myself. Don't give me that look. You know I've been using birth control."

"I know what you tell me."

*"I'm going to forget you said that. You're disap-
pointed. I had plans too. Things happen, Joe. We can be
happy about this. You always said you wanted—"*

*"When I was ready, Marilyn. I said when I was
ready."*

"It's your first son or daughter."

"That's not fair."

"Neither is the fact that I'm pregnant."

So Little Joey came out from between his mother's am-
bivalent thighs into his father's resentful arms. He forced
himself on their lives, like some crazy seed determined to
root itself in sand. Dutifully, they tended the plant, hoping to
grow the comfort they needed. The gardening consumed
them, ate their days. Broke their backs. The necessary work.
The longing for the flower before its time. The hands
stretched, ached, reached . . .

Once they held champagne, stoked a fireplace, willingly
stroked skin that wanted to be touched, held warmth to
warmth. This was it. Joe was no knight in shining armor, but
he treated her right.

Besides, she'd known him for five years. He'd met her
when she was working in the biology research department of
a pharmaceutical company. Those were the days when

Marilyn believed she could do anything, even discover the cure for cancer.

Joe was brash, blond, pigheaded. Sometimes she'd run into him on Fridays, when he came into the office in his three-piece and shiny shoes. He carried a briefcase like all the other sales reps, but Marilyn believed he wasn't like all the others. He wasn't what you'd call handsome. He had energy, charm. He was going to night school, studying business management.

They'd lie in bed many nights just talking. Dreaming. She'd see a research institute in her name, humming with men and women doing important work to save lives. He was a CEO somewhere, making billion-dollar decisions. It was a wonderful dream.

She followed it down the aisle of holy matrimony. So did Little Joey. He was born eight months later.

She kept waiting for everything to go back to normal, back to the time of dreaming. It never did. Joe had to drop out of school and work two jobs. Marilyn found herself in a surreal state. She suffered from sleep deprivation. The only things that brought her to for a moment were the minute-to-minute demands of the creature that had come out of her. It was as if the baby had been magnified while she'd been miniaturized, lost in the world of her apartment. She couldn't cry out for help. No one would hear her. She learned to sleepwalk through her days. Time passed unnoticed, until a hand reached down to help her. It was an offer to teach at the local college. She grabbed it.

So here she was.

It isn't that she doesn't love Little Joey. That, in fact, is the problem.

Marilyn makes it through the day, as usual. She finishes teaching, grades some papers. Her work life ends at four-thirty. As she drives across campus, the world darkens. Her car moves down the highway, over side streets, past shopkeepers rolling up their awnings for the night. She returns home.

The dream recurs that night. Beneath her cool, clean sheets, it patiently awaits her. This night, it is different.

Soft blues interwoven with itchy, static gray. She is in her old lab coat. She jumps from the terrace as soon as Joey falls. With everything she has, she tries to reach him. She tries to find his hand. But something keeps pulling her up, away from him, higher, into the clouds. Finally, she can no longer see him.

She is sick. She has lost Joey. She has failed. Her lab coat is gone. Facedown, arms spread out, her body begins to fall. She tries to drown herself in the air. Deserves it. To die. She senses, instead, that she is moving, upward.

Slowly. She is being lifted. She feels her heart pulsing in her fingers. She rises. No Little Joey. She rises. No Joe. Nothing but white, crisp, white clouds. Her body is wonderful. It does anything she asks it to. Each cloud wipes her eyes and kisses her as she glides up, up into the soft ocean sky.

When Marilyn awakens, she is squeezing Little Joey's blue sock. Her nightgown is covered with tears and sweat.

Saturday afternoon. Marilyn is sitting in her neighbor Ginny's living room. She is surrounded by wood. Empty, colonial. There are smooth, polished surfaces, everything in its place. Ginny is in the bathroom. Marilyn plays with the diamond wedding ring on her finger, desperate for just one moment of peace. She can hear Joey crying across the hall, in her kitchen, while Joe sleeps. This is one of those days when he can't breathe without her. Everywhere she goes, there he is.

Ginny seems to have it all figured out. Preschool twins and a toddler. Three kids and barely a trace of them. Marilyn decides that either Ginny is dropping Valium into their cereal or spending every waking moment cleaning all the corners of her house. She is happy when her eyes spot a yellow building block under the couch.

"Beautiful day, huh?" Ginny says, bouncing into the

room. A tiny rivulet of sweat is beginning on her forehead, beneath her stylish red hair. She is vibrant in a black and gold one-piece.

Marilyn is wearing a flowered housecoat, feeling like a menopausal whale stuck in a hot flash. "Yeah. Nice," she says.

"Danny and Donny are at tap class, and Mary just fell off to sleep." Her big, satisfied grin makes Marilyn want to throw up all over the furniture.

"Uh-huh. Look, Ginny . . ." She pushes her hair back in a gesture of absolute fatigue.

Ginny's face sours. "What's wrong, kid?"

Kid. She hates that habit of hers, calling her "kid."

"Nothing. Nothing's wrong, Ginny. Joe thinks I'm over here borrowing a cup of sugar. What I really need is a bowl of peace and quiet. Don't tell me you couldn't hear Joey crying all morning."

"That? Doesn't ever bother me."

"C'mon. Your kids don't get on your nerves?"

"They're babies. Whatever they feel, they want us to feel too. Sort of primal, don't you think? Like Henry and I were sharing just last night—"

Marilyn rises from the sofa. "I really do have to go. Can't be away from my Joey too long. You know how it is."

"Sure. I understand. See ya."

As soon as Marilyn turns the doorknob of her apartment, she hears delighted squeals. Little Joey's puffy face greets her as she steps into the foyer.

"Mommy! Mommy!"

He looks like he's been crying every day of his life.

"I told you Mommy was coming back. I just had to get something, sweetie."

Chocolate stains are smeared across his lips and down his once-white undershirt. His cartoon-covered underpants are at his knees. Beneath the crumpled jeans around his ankles are the shoelaces he has found a way to untie. The remains of sticky, red candy is on his fingers.

Talking fast, he grabs her hand and leads her to the bathroom. "Look. All clean."

Toilet paper is on top of his potty, in the toilet, in streams across the sink and bathtub, in wet clumps and dry piles all over the floor.

"I clean up. See, Mommy?"

Marilyn places her hand on her forehead and closes her eyes.

"See, Mommy? I help. Love you"—his arms are open wide—"this big."

He pokes his lips out. "Hug? Hug kiss?"

Marilyn breathes deeply. She cannot resist him. She gathers his tiny body into her breasts and holds him tight.

Monday morning. Early. A cup of coffee before the world outside her home awakens. She can't see it clearly, but looking down, out of her kitchen window, she thinks there is an exotic bird in the courtyard tree. She opens her curtains wider. Her head moves. Her eyes search the tree for what she thinks she saw.

There it is. A shower of brilliant red orange on the leaves. The colors shine, sparkle, dance. Marilyn cannot wait for the elevator. She takes the stairs and walks out into the courtyard. She looks for the shining. She moves slowly, toward the tree. She doesn't want to scare the beauty away.

She spots the bird. Up close, it has no colors, no light. Common. Ordinary. Same little brown speckled bird she sees day in, day out. Brilliance only memory. For one moment, though, shimmering glints of sunlight had made it extraordinary. Slowly, she turns and goes back upstairs.

Wait.

Donny is crying. "Didn't I tell you? Hold still or Mommy will make it hurt more," Ginny says. "No. No hug for you. Get off of me, Donny. Mommy doesn't love you when you don't behave. Bad, bad Donny." Donny is crying and crying as if he cannot stop.

Marilyn is queasy. She feels like she has heard something she wasn't supposed to hear.

She goes quietly into her apartment. Enters her kitchen. Her coffee is cold. Slowly, she sits down on her chair. Once seated, she feels uncertain of where to place her feet. She shifts her weight and looks back toward the kitchen window. Little Joey startles her, his quick footsteps coming toward her, as he awakens.

After work, Marilyn is blessed to enter a quiet home once again.

"Joey's asleep," Joe tells her, along with his kiss on the way out the door.

Silence.

Marilyn is exhausted, but afraid to sleep. The silence fills her with an ocean of her thoughts. She has spent the day standing far from the shore, pretending there was no salty blue, white froth, uncontrollable, surging, rising.

It happens quickly. She is cramping, grabbing the edge of the kitchen table. The pain is eating its way through her pelvis, burning a path to the top of her head. *The baby*. Tears fall onto her hands and slide between her fingers.

Hold on. Don't look down.

She leans heavily on her palms, feeling the burden shift. Her legs weaken and sway. Marilyn sees herself lying unconscious. She fights to stand up.

I'm here.

She faces the pain, until she feels it give in. Slowly. Slowly.

Tears drip off her chin.

Mama's here.

The teardrops make bright, clear spots on the table. Her breathing deepens. Holding her arms crossed against her stomach, she sits and rocks.

Marilyn doesn't remember finding the bed, dreaming. She is awake for a moment. Breathing. Little Joey is wrapped around her. The baby powder smell of him is in her nose. His hair falls across her face as he kisses her cheeks, her nose, her forehead. She is falling. Deeper, deeper, surrendering to a bottomless well filled with his love. Their light. Nothing else matters. One hand in Joey's, one on her belly, she falls asleep to the stirrings of new life inside her. Joe will be home soon. A thought vibrates. *I will tell him in the morning.*

Jarvis

The bus is so cold. He snuggles up into the seat as best he can, trying to ignore the draft coming from the metal vent along the window. His feet are numb, his legs cramped. The woman next to him is babbling on about her son in med school.

Jarvis's gut shivers. The trembling is a long-handled itch his breathing cannot scratch. Stale cigarette smoke gurgles raw in his throat. His hand is shaking as he feels for his back pocket. Mama's baby. He longs for her warm, wet kisses on his forehead. He finds the business card Daddy gave him a few days ago. A friend who might be able to get him a job. He feeds himself from his glass bottle.

There, there, my sweet darlin'. S-h-h-h.

Mama?

I'm your father. I'm not gonna baby you like your mama. You're a grown man now.

Mama?

Hush little baby, don't say a word . . . That's my sweet, baby boy . . .

He is all tingly and full. The cheap liquid, hot inside him. He is on his way. This time it will be different. This time.

Gonna be a bum all your life, son?

The bus rocks him gently in its groove along the highway. He is going somewhere. Finally, he is going . . .

Sleep now, my sugar baby. Sleep.

Jarvis's head snaps back against the greasy headrest. From far off, a voice is shaking his shoulder.

"Mister. Mister. This the last stop."

"Huh?"

"New York. We're in New York."

Alright.

The city screams at him. Everything is alive. His heart pumps uncontrollably, simmering in his chest. The street air tickles his cheek, as Jarvis spits on the concrete beneath him. His hair is mussed. A chestnut-colored strand of it falls, un-curling onto his forehead. He is almost handsome. Soft tar eyes and a nose broken too many times, in one too many kick-start jukebox joints.

He rests his duffel bag on the ground and pulls the card out of his pocket. "George Fredricksen, Corporate Law." This is the man Daddy says is going to save him, turn his life around. He sips in the sights around him. Thin, pink lips slightly open. He trembles. The icy-fingered wind slips in between the buttons of his unlined coat, raising the hairs on his arms, his chest, his legs. Montgomery was never this cold in April.

He gathers his coat around him, standing there in the middle of the sidewalk, waiting. His toes are electric. Something is supposed to happen. He looks across the street. There is a bar on the other side, a quiet darkness, inviting him in. Slinging his bag over his shoulder, Jarvis decides to cross. He moves between the flashing, metal teeth of cars, trucks, and bikes.

He enters the bar, heads toward the bathroom.

"Only for customers," the pock-faced bartender scowls. "You gonna piss or drink?"

Jarvis smiles and keeps on walking toward the bathroom door. "I reckon I'll do both. Bourbon. Straight up."

He returns after a few minutes, downs his bourbon, and orders another. He should call. He unbuttons his coat and looks out the window.

Old men, garbage-smudged, open-palmed, take part in a ritual, a chanting for copper, for silver, to fill their hands, drop by drop, turn metal into glass, bury themselves beneath one bottle after another.

Girls trapped early, firmly, inside hard women's edges. Lace stockings, purple heels, cheap yellow pumps, shiny boots. They are nervous racehorses pacing in front of their starting gates. Some lean toward car windows, behinds pressed in by imitation leather skirts hanging beneath jackets that don't look warm enough.

"Mr. Fredricksen?"

Swollen-ankled people yell down crowded streets, their hair lice and soot matted, as they argue with buddies long gone—friends forever no one else can see, comrades hammered too often, too deeply, by each of life's losses.

Women. Exquisite women who Jarvis imagines wear their jewelry like perfume, place it delicately between their breasts, splash their wrists with gems, trickle gold and rubies down their fingers, drip diamonds from their earlobes. Cabs whisk them away, back to satin sheets and the men who can afford them.

Limousines slide to the curb. Chauffeurs pop out, open doors. Trench-coated businessmen appear, pudgy hands complete with wedding bands and watches, tightly gripping briefcases, disappearing into office-layered skyscrapers.

"Tomorrow. Ten o'clock is fine."

These Northerners. Different. Different rhythm. Different faces. But the feeling . . . He knows it. The feeling has followed him through the backwoods of his mouth and gut, like old Jefferson, his mutt, wet-nosed, leading him. In this someplace new, he has found his same old spot.

Jarvis tries to concentrate on today and tomorrow. They are fading, like the bourbon rising from his tongue. He digs into his pockets, orders another drink, then slowly slides down the sides of his shot glass, collecting himself in the dark brown circle at the bottom.

Free

I knew before I got the phone call that morning that Mama had died.

They said she was five feet six inches tall and weighed two hundred and fifty-eight pounds at the time of her death. It happened in the back of a white and orange ambulance before the strangers, who were her last image, could get her to the hospital. She had exactly eleven dollars and thirty-two cents in her pocketbook and nothing in the bank.

Her heart just quit. Failure, they called it. But *I* knew that at sixty-seven, she had simply run out of beats, could no longer think of new ways to pump life through all the cells that kept her spirit chained. Just plain tired of being tired.

I stood in the middle of the living room floor, the telephone receiver, this inanimate thing that had given me the message, pressed between my hand and my thigh. When the first wave of tears hit me, I thought I too would die. I wanted to. With the second wave, something snapped and crumbled inside my chest. Mama.

It is the last period before the end of the day. I am thirteen, in gym class. None of the white boys want to hold my hand. There are children around me waiting for a signal from Miss Shannon, our teacher, so they can begin square dancing.

No one wants to hold my hand. I squeeze my mouth, making my lips disappear. I stare at the spot at the top of the bleachers where Daddy and I sat on Wednesday night, watching Georgette, my big sister, play for the school team.

"Paula?" Miss Shannon asks.

My throat is slowly filling up with tears. There are no words. I will not cry—not here. Miss Shannon takes one look at me and says I am excused. I spend the rest of class watching them, hating them. I tuck my tears safely away where no one can see. I am saving them for Mama. Only she will know what to do.

Walking home, sidewalks, people, colors melt to gray and press against the wetness on my cheeks. I race up the concrete steps to my house. Somehow Mama already knows and meets me at the door. I enter.

Eyes closed as she squeezes me against her, I enter. Inside her again, warm and protected. Always her baby. Always. Her baby.

I lay on the floor, my body curled into itself. I cried myself to sleep.

It was ninety degrees on the day of the funeral. Pushing

myself out of bed was hard. Standing in front of the mirror fully dressed was harder. I didn't want to go. I didn't want to get dressed up. Why did I have to look my best when I felt my worst? My sadness was so deep that I couldn't hold on to it. A slippery, formless thing inside me that wouldn't stay still long enough for me to shake it loose. One minute I didn't think I could keep it together. The next, I couldn't feel a thing. Surrendering, I closed the top button of my blouse and walked out the front door.

My sisters and I entered the church together. I itched with all the eyes that were upon us. Georgette, long braids down her back, face dark, smooth and stunning even in grief, was wearing a plain black dress. Allen, her boyish-faced husband, looked helpless, his arm awkwardly around her, as their three teenage sons walked solemnly behind.

I felt like I was suffocating in the black blouse and skirt I'd dug out of the back of my closet. My younger sister, Linda, puffy-eyed, overweight, and armed with Kleenex, wore an expensive two-piece brown suit that brought out the maple tones in her skin. For a second, I thought she was Mama. I had to close my eyes and open them again.

A memory replayed itself of Mama out of breath and sweating in the middle of fall. Having outgrown Dad a long time ago, she hadn't remarried in thirty years. No man would ever tell her what to do again. Unable to keep a job for long without letting her supervisor know a thing or two, she borrowed money when she needed to and took odd jobs whenever she could.

She looked disoriented as she trudged in her boots up Georgette's driveway, struggling against a wave that only she could see. Loaded down with a shopping bag and a big pocketbook across her shoulder, her brown skirt was hanging beneath her winter coat. It was one of our better Thanksgivings.

"Here she comes," Georgette said, sighing. She opened the door. "Ma, so glad you could make it. You look great!" she said as she gave Mama a quick kiss and hug.

There were dark lines under Mama's eyes. "Uh-huh. Some things you'll need," she said, handing Georgette the bag.

"Mama, you do look good," I insisted.

The whole house held its breath. You never knew what was going to come out of Mama's mouth. Since she left Dad, the people around her had either been frightened of her or embarrassed by her.

"You all can say what you want"—Mama lifted her arm so Linda could help her with her coat—"I know how

I look. Been in this bag a bones for sixty-six years now."
She plopped into the nearest chair. "Your father. He
married a skinny little girl. Been gone a long time. Don't
know why everybody always wanna sugarcoat the truth.
For Chrissake, take a bite out of it. Don't ever taste bad as
it looks."

Linda reached out and squeezed my hand. I squeezed
back and took a deep breath. We moved toward the space that
had been cleared for us in the front.

I took my seat. I noticed that the casket was closed.
Something was gently pulling my eyes to the right. It was
Mama. She was up front, standing near the podium, smiling
down at me.

She was a teenager again, with a red, red shade of fifties
lipstick. Her grin carried me from one end of her dark
caramel face to the other. Mama had on the orange and red
patterned dress I'd seen her wearing once in our family al-
bum. The Indian in her was strong—her long, black hair
shining like the brilliance in her eyes. White gloves. Her
impish hands were on her devilish hips, while the minister,
somber in his black majesty, readied himself for his big
number.

I tried to muffle my laugh. Georgette leaned forward
from her end of the pew, scorching a path through the others

until her eyes lit into mine. How could I be laughing at a time like this?

But Mama was up there. She was all of us—Georgette's beauty, Linda's tenderness, my rebelliousness. Her gifts were clear. Her time on earth complete.

I looked to the left at Linda, across the aisle at Dad. No reaction.

It was difficult listening to the preacher. I kept hearing Mama's voice editing his script. He was reading from the Bible. She was reciting poetry from the 60's. He was using righteous words to milk God's holy tears from his congregation. She was telling me whose wife he milked at three o'clock this morning.

I tried to control myself, but I couldn't hold back the laugh that was rolling all the way up from my toes. It came out as a scream.

The part of the congregation I could see was staring at me when I looked up. I immediately broke into tears, hoping they'd think I was hysterical. I was. Now it was Linda's turn.

"Girl? You okay?" she asked, more embarrassed than concerned.

"Yeah," I said, laughing, then covering my mouth.

Georgette rose and smiled at all the faces. She walked gracefully over and crouched down in front of me. Her smile died as she looked at my face. So only I could hear her, she said, "Look, I don't know what's going on with you, Paula. But I expect you, as a member of this family, to respect Mama's memory."

I didn't bother to try and explain. My eyes followed Georgette's walk back to her seat as I heard the soloist sing.

I sing because I'm happy, I sing because I'm free . . .

I sensed Mama again. I could touch her in the air. The notes from all the songs inside her were sprinkled against the gloom.

Aunt Dahlia's hat slid to the right, making her look like the gangster she really was. Dad's zipper refused to stay up, just like the old days, under the stairwell, when Mama and Daddy were kids. Miriam, Dad's fourth wife, couldn't stop her heel and toe from tapping out a staccato beat.

The ushers opened the casket. It was time to file past. I felt Mama next to me. I stood up to get in line. A minty feeling flooded my chest. Overflowing joy, Mama touched me. The warmest, most peaceful hug resonated through my body. I closed my eyes and felt gentle kisses on my cheeks and neck. Someone put a tissue in my hand. I never saw the corpse.

The recessional played as we walked outside the church.

The pallbearers placed the flowered load into the back of the limousine.

I began walking away.

"Paula, where are you going?" Linda asked.

"Not now, Paula. Don't do this now," Georgette commanded.

I stopped, but didn't turn around. I loved Mama. Was I disgracing her by not going to the cemetery?

The bones and flesh inside the expensive metal box had nothing to do with her. I had no interest in watching that box lowered into the ground.

Still tingling from the hug inside the church, I needed time to think. I kept walking.

"Paula!" Georgette screamed.

Someone sniffled, and said, "Let her go."

I got into my car and put on a tape of Mama's favorite song. I held on to the steering wheel, breathing the music in. Feeling it vibrate first down my throat, then slowly filling my lungs. "Mama," I said, laughing. Leaning the seat back, I let the music take me.

Cars were lining up behind the limo. Their lights were on. I closed my eyes. In the darkness, Mama covered me. I was inside her again. I lay still. My heart locking softly into hers, giving her the beat. What would always be there flowed between us, as she washed me in my tears.

I took a cleansing breath, felt the song in my lungs. I turned the motor on and put the car in drive to pull off from the curb. Still humming, I patted my thigh.

We'll be dancin'
Dancin' in the streets . . .

I watched the silent funeral procession pass by, then I went the other way.

E p i l o g u e

"All them stories. You seen something didn't you, boy?" Old Angel asked Young One. "Good."

Together they sat at the edge of a cloud and peeked down. They looked at the huge, ancient prison where so many guarded themselves, some never seeing the walls and bars they had neatly fashioned into the everyday. Some believing they were born bound, were filling their hands thick with chains, while others were shape-shifting infinitely slipping shackle after shackle . . .

Young One sat staring, fascinated, overwhelmed.

Old Angel touched him on his shoulder. "My work is finished," he said. "My time is up."

The change was under way. He could feel Young One passing through him, dissolving from image to emotion to distant remembrance. Old Angel was beginning anew, going below, perhaps this time as white, as woman. He would give up the memory of his wings, all but one feather, and one day, find his way back home . . .